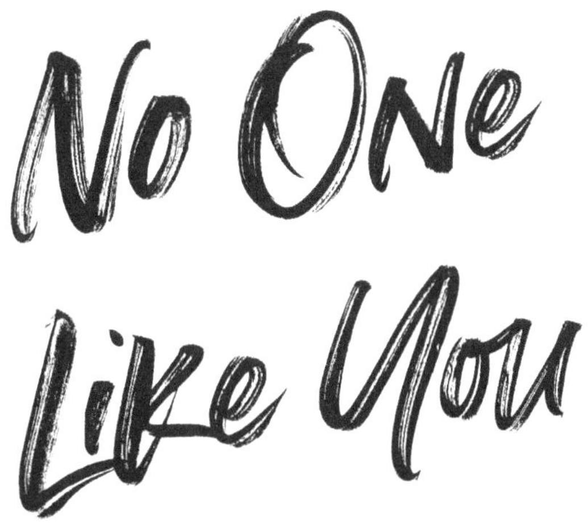

CHRIS WALTERS

ISBN: 978-1-964292-00-7
eISBN: 978-1-964292-01-4

CONTENTS

CHAPTER 1
THE ROAD TO NOWHERE

Megan Kowalski pulled over next to an overlook as she struggled to breathe. She tried desperately to remember her exercises; the basics of deep calming breaths that she had taught her students for years. More than anything, Megan wanted to keep it together for the sake of Sophia, who was sitting anxiously in the passenger seat.

As she watched the setting sun turn the slopes of Mt. Hood a beautiful golden pink, Megan tried to think of some sort of plan. Today should have been easy. It was the Friday before Thanksgiving, which meant a short week and small class sizes ahead of her. But Sophia had forgotten her roller skates that morning, so Megan decided to run home during her planning period. And that was when her life came crashing down.

Brad's truck is here. He didn't say anything about leaving work early today. I remember he said that his battery was acting up. Maybe the truck didn't start today and he got a ride with someone.

Megan didn't call out when she entered their home. Sophia's room was on the ground floor and she picked up the roller skates when she heard a thump from upstairs. Megan tentatively ascended the staircase, wishing that she had a baseball bat or some other weapon.

Maybe Brad stained his clothes at lunch and came home to change. That's probably it.

Wait… Was that a moan?

Megan crept forward toward the open bedroom door. She heard moaning ahead, from two different voices. Looking through the door, she saw Brad's naked back between a pair of outstretched legs. Sophia's roller skates fell from Megan's nerveless hands, and the crash as they hit the floor alerted Brad and his paramour to Megan's presence. Megan remembered how Brad and the woman desperately tried to cover themselves with both sheets and lies.

This wasn't the first time he had cheated on her, but it sure as hell would be the last. She could forgive Brad's indiscretions once, but not again. Megan told him that she was leaving him and that she was taking Sophia with her. Brad begged her to stay as she haphazardly threw clothing into bags for herself and Sophia. He promised that this particular mistake would never be repeated, trying to plead and bargain his way out of his mistakes.

"That's what you promised the last time," she had told him.

"I'm sorry, it really won't happen again, I swear," Brad insisted.

For Megan, it was too late, and Brad's promises were as worthless as his marriage vows. So there she was, parked on the side of a state highway with her eight-year-old daughter, headed vaguely toward Portland with no idea what to do next.

Megan's body memory kicked in, and the breathing exercises took hold. Four beats in. Four beats hold. Four beats out. Four beats hold. Repeat. It might not fully quell a panic attack, but it could take the edge off a bit.

"Mommy, why are we stopped?" Sophia asked.

"Because the view is beautiful," she replied. And it was. The Cascades got a lot of rain in the fall, and at high altitudes that meant a good amount of snow to reflect the alpenglow. On a sunny day, it was breathtaking.

"Are we going home soon?"

"No, sweetie. Your dad and I… We… I… I'm sorry, we're not going home tonight. I don't know when. I'm… I'm sorry, sweetheart."

Megan licked her lips, tasting the faint salt of dried tears mixed with the acridness of her streaked mascara. She really needed a plan. She could try a hotel, but that was expensive, especially this close to a major holiday—if her credit cards even still worked. All of her cards were registered in both of their names—as a supposed sign of trust—so Brad might have already canceled them. Now that she thought about it, she suspected that Brad probably had other cards that she didn't know about.

Shaking her head to stop from going down that particular rabbit hole, Megan tried to focus on the task at hand. Sleeping in the car was out of the question. The cold would be nearly unbearable, and the questions from Sophia would be even worse. Megan did have friends back at home, but they were all mutual friends with Brad. Word would eventually get around—like it always did in small towns—but Megan didn't want to announce their family problems to the whole town by asking to spend the night.

"Did I do something wrong?" Sophia asked.

"No, sweetheart, you didn't! This is something between me and your father." She reached over to squeeze her daughter's hand.

Suddenly she thought of someone who might help—Tasha! Tasha moved to Portland a few years back for a job. Something with computer graphics. After being roommates in college for four years, Tasha had been her maid of honor. For a few years after she got married, Megan and Tasha had communicated often, but as the years went on they slowly lost touch. Calls became emails, emails became the occasional text, and now she mailed Tasha the annual family Christmas letter, but that was about it. *Here goes nothing,* Megan said to herself, and she reached for her phone.

CHAPTER 2
YOU'VE GOT A FRIEND IN ME

Tasha Washington was busy working—and she was probably going to be working overtime again—when her phone rang. She was deep in the zone, Taylor Swift in her headphones helping her stay focused, so she didn't answer it at first. When the phone rang again, she actually looked at the screen and was surprised to see her old roommate calling. Pausing Taylor mid-song, Tasha reached over and swiped right.

"Hey, Megan! It's been a minute!"

"Tasha! I'm sorry to call, and I know that you're probably busy, and I know that this is inconvenie—"

"Slow down! What's going on?"

"I need help, Tasha. I don't know who else to turn to, and I'm desperate. I know this is probably a bad time—I'm sure you're busy."

"Megan! Okay, slow down again. What's going on? What do you need?"

There was a pause, and then Megan whispered, "I caught Brad cheating on me. I took Sophia and left."

"What? Wait, let me turn up my phone. What was that?"

"I caught Brad cheating on me and I took Sophia and left."

"What an asshole! I told you that you should have left him the first time!"

Her voice must have carried, because she heard Sophia ask, "Mommy, who are you talking to?"

"I'm talking to your Aunt Tasha, sweetie."

After Megan answered her daughter's question, she responded to Tasha. "I know, and now I know that you were right. I guess I thought that he could change, and I was wrong."

"Well, I won't say that I told you so… oh, wait, I guess I just did." Tasha looked around to see if any of her co-workers—or worse, her boss—were paying attention. Seeing that no one was eavesdropping, she continued. "Sorry. Ummmm, so you said that you left the lying, cheating little shitweasel. Where are you now?"

"I'm south of Mt. Hood. I've been driving for a while, but I don't know where I'm going or what I'm going to do. I thought about hotels, but I don't know if my cards will still work, and it's expensive, and—"

"Megan! You're spiraling! That's okay, you've had a tough day. The two of you can crash at my place for a night or two and we'll figure something out."

"No, that's too much! I can't ask you to do that. Do you know of any shelters or anything?"

"Bitch, please… we spent four years in the same room, and, you ain't askin', I'm offering. Actually, I'm not offering. I'm *telling* you that you and Sophia are staying with me.

"Are you sure?"

"Of course, I'm sure. It's gonna be cozy, but we'll make it work. Plus, I haven't seen that little munchkin in years. I bet that she looks just like you now," Tasha said. Taking a deep breath to center herself, Tasha asked, "Do you need my address?"

"Yes, thank you. Please text it to me. I owe you, big time!"

Tasha heard Megan start to choke up. "I'm pretty sure that we both owe each other a lot from our college days, so we'll call it even. I'll text you my address. Give me a call again when you get close, okay?"

"Thank you again. I'll call you soon."

"See you soon!" Tasha ended the call and immediately started a mental priority list for what needed to be done at her apartment. She hopped on to Slack and messaged Kevin that she had an emergency and needed to leave immediately, then grabbed her coat and dashed to the elevator. As the elevator doors slid shut, she heard her boss yelling her name from across the office. Tasha knew that he would be pissed and would find new and inventive ways to make her miserable. As she texted Megan her address, she got the first of many increasingly angry texts from her boss. *Fuck that guy and this job*, Tasha thought. *If I didn't need the damn insurance, I would be out of here.* Kevin was a problem for later.

Tasha pulled up her ride-share app and balked at the surge pricing. It wasn't *that* much faster than the bus, so the bus it was. Thankfully, Trimet ran frequently this time of day, and she only had to wait a couple of minutes. As she sat down, that mental priority list came back into focus. She had a lot to do, but hopefully, she'd have enough time to clean up and at least start some laundry. Luckily, there weren't too many stops, and now she had a plan of action.

Of course, like most plans, it fell apart as soon as Tasha closed her apartment door. She could hear the meows start the moment her key touched the lock—Nocturne was thrilled that her human was home early. Tasha was greeted with a veritable whirlwind of head bonks, meows, and purrs, followed by the classic fall-over-and-roll-around-adorably maneuver. She spent a couple of precious minutes scratching and cooing at her feline roommate before slipping off her coat. It wasn't news to Tasha that cleaning up or even moving around could be challenging when a cat decided to "help," but in this particular moment, it was extra distracting. She nearly tripped more than once and got rewarded with an outraged squeak when Nocturne decided to move right where her foot was going. Even so, she had her apartment in mostly presentable shape by the time her phone rang. Tasha's heart fell as she saw the 14 unread messages from Kevin, plus the

Slack notifications, and the icon representing unread emails that she just knew were the harbinger of yet more misery. But that was something she'd worry about later.

Taking a deep breath to calm herself, she answered her phone. "Hey, Megan! How far away are you?"

"Hi, Aunt Tasha! Mom says that we are about thirty minutes from your address."

"Aw, Sophia. I'm so looking forward to seeing you and your mom. You tell her to drive safe, and I'll see you both soon, okay?"

"Okay, Aunt Tasha! Bye!"

Tasha set down her phone and opened up her laptop. Pulling up the website of the Thai place down the street, she ordered what she hoped would be a good selection. It would be ready with hopefully just enough time for her to walk over and pick it up before Megan and Sophia arrived.

She was just getting back to her apartment when a green Subaru pulled in across the street. She didn't immediately recognize the blonde woman in the driver's seat, but underneath the curly mop of red hair in the passenger seat was almost certainly her goddaughter, Sophia.

CHAPTER 3

CRYING IN THE RAIN

Megan set the parking brake, turned off the car, and looked up to see a tall figure at the door of the apartment building across the street. She immediately recognized her friend, and her stomach growled when she noticed what looked like a big bag of takeout. She helped Sophia with her seat belt and pulled the door handle. Opening the door and standing up, she called Tasha's name. Sophia streaked across the street, yelling Tasha's name at the top of her lungs. Tasha was awkwardly balancing the takeout food with one arm, the eight-year-old wrapped around her waist, as Megan walked up. Megan could feel the tears starting again, mixing with the evening drizzle that was shifting into Portland's seasonally ubiquitous light rain.

"Thank you so much, Tasha! I don't know what we would have done without you."

"Megan, shush. It's what friends do. And what the hell did you do to your hair? Blonde?"

"Always focusing on what's important. That's the same old Tasha."

"Come on, let's get you two inside, then we can get your bags or whatever. After that, we'll get you dry, and we can eat."

Tasha led them up a flight of stairs and down a hall. Opening up the door, she said, "We're home now and this is…" Tasha looked for Nocturne, but the cat was nowhere to be seen. "Well, I guess that someone decided to be shy. Y'all will meet Nocturne soon enough, I suppose."

"Who is, Nock… Noc–?" Sophia asked.

"Nocturne. She's my cat. I hope that y'all aren't allergic, are you?"

"Not as far as I know," Megan responded.

"That's good to hear. Let's hope it stays that way, or this might be awkward. Sophia, let me show you where the forks and plates are, and you can get dinner set up on the table while me and your mom go back to the car, all right?"

"Okay, Aunt Tasha."

"I'll hang your coat up, and we'll be right back."

Once they were out in the hallway, Megan turned to Tasha and said, "Thank you again. Are you sure that this is all right? We're not messing with any Friday night plans, are we?"

"Nah, I was just gonna Netflix and chill with Nocturne tonight."

"No hot date? Look at you… I mean, maybe not in sweatpants, but… Oh… God… Oh, you were busy cleaning for us. I'm so sorry!"

"Megan… chill, okay? I jetted out of work early to tidy up a bit. Kevin's mad… that's my boss. He's *such* an asshole. But screw him, you're way more important to me."

"I'm sorry, Tasha. I'm such a mess and you're putting yourself out for us and I've been a bad friend the past few years." Megan started crying again, and she hated herself for it. Then she felt Tasha's arms embrace her, and one hand came up to gently stroke her hair.

"It's okay, Megan. It takes two to tango, or in this case, not tango. I should have been better about calling you, too. Y'all are here now and that's what's important. You'll get through this, I promise."

"I don't know if anything will ever be okay again. I trusted

Brad. I thought we were in a good place. Well, maybe not a good place, but a decent place. Certainly not a place where he would be cheating on me. Did you know that he introduced me to that woman at his company picnic last summer? Oh, her husband, too. And now I'm here; we're here. How do I explain this to Sophia? I don't want her to hate her own father, even if I really hate him now. Is it something that I did? Was I not good enough for him?"

"Hey, slow down. You gotta breathe. Breathe in for four beats, then hold."

Megan couldn't help but laugh. "That's exactly what I used to tell my students."

"Oh, so you know then! Just breathe, and we'll get through this. This isn't on you. Brad is a cheating bastard and that's his fault, not yours. We'll talk it out. I can tell that you're a good mom, and you'll figure out the right thing to say to Sophia. And sweetie, we *have* to do something about this hair. Why the hell did you ever go blonde?"

"Stop it. I can't have a good cry about my pain if you keep making me laugh."

"I keep hearing that laughter is the best medicine or something like that. Now let's get your bags and get you fed because your stomach is gonna wake up this whole building soon."

Megan reached up to dry her eyes. That brief moment of human contact with someone, especially after today, made her feel a lot better. As they descended the stairs, Megan felt, for the first time since she'd walked into her former home that afternoon, that things could maybe be all right, eventually.

"I went blonde because I thought that Brad would like it. In retrospect, maybe brunette would have been a better choice." With a slightly bitter laugh, she added, "Oof, that hurt to say, but it didn't hurt as badly as I thought."

"Well, that's a good start, then. You can go back to red if you want, or if you want something different, I know someone who can help you go another direction."

"Another direction? Like what? Strawberry blonde?"

"Nah… I'm thinking purple… or green… or maybe hot pink. Or if you go red, go like fire truck red."

"Uhhhh, I don't know, Tasha. That might be a bit much right now."

"Yeah, but it could also be the right amount of 'much' right now. Just sayin'! Also, we're going to need to move your car in the morning. I know some places nearby where you don't need to pay for parking."

As they got back to the apartment, the smell of warm Thai food invaded Megan's nostrils. She felt like she hadn't eaten in a week.

"I don't know what you like these days, so I got a mix of stuff. Pad Thai, chicken and broccoli, there's some vegetarian fried rice, and uh… the drunken noodles. I figure that the fried rice or the chicken and broccoli would be good for Sophia because they aren't spicy."

"Thanks, Aunt Tasha! I like it spicy, but not as spicy as Mom. Daddy doesn't like spicy food, though."

Tasha leaned in and whispered, "See, that should have been a sign. As soon as he choked on that chili I made our senior year, you shoulda run, girl."

"Yeah, yeah. You always told me that I was the only white girl that you'd invite to a family barbecue."

"You still are." Tahsa's expression was strained as if there were more that she wasn't sharing.

"Hey, are you okay?"

"It's okay. Long story. Let's focus on getting you and your girl fed right now. Then you can sleep, or talk or whatever. I know that you've had a long day."

"Sounds good! I hope that you like the Pad Thai because that drunken noodle is all mine."

"Oh no, we are splitting that! And don't give me those puppy dog eyes! Sophia, you know that your mom doesn't play fair, right?"

"Can I try that drunken noodle?"

"Oh, sweetie, of course," Megan and Tasha said at once.

"Jinx!" they both said, and for a brief moment they laughed, and it was like no time had passed at all.

The meal was amazing, although the only thing Megan really remembered about it was that it tasted good. Once Sophia was in bed, Megan and Tasha sat down on the couch and started talking. As exhausted as Megan was, it felt so good to reconnect with Tasha. Their conversation rambled from life to politics to food to movies and beyond. It was just like those long nights in college, talking across a dark room from their beds, just without the sounds of drunken vomiting outside. Eventually though, Megan must have drifted off. She vaguely sensed being guided to bed before oblivion overtook her.

CHAPTER 4
THE BEST

Megan surfaced from slumber and had a nearly immediate panic attack. Even with her eyes still closed, she could tell that this wasn't her bed, there was someone else in it, and she had an incredibly intense cramp in her legs. Then, yesterday's events came crashing down on her. Catching Brad with another woman, the fight, taking Sophia, the drive to Portland, and then seeing Tasha for the first time in years. *Tasha! Oh no! Okay. Relax, breathe.* Megan opened her eyes, which seemed like much more of a struggle than normal, especially for a Saturday. The red hair peeking from under the blankets identified Sophia as her bedmate.

That didn't explain the dead weight behind her knees, though. Gingerly lifting herself, she spotted a little black mound tucked in the crook of her legs. From that mound, a tiny head lifted up, opened its eyes, and squeaked in protest at her movement. The mound unfolded itself into a cat, who proceeded to then stretch in the infuriatingly luxurious manner of their kind.

Megan knew that despite a decade or so of yoga, she would never achieve the exquisite bliss that this cat's stretches promised. This must be Nocturne.

Nocturne, after being rudely awakened, stalked off in a huff through the door. Megan followed, although not as quickly, as her legs took a bit more coaxing as blood rushed back in. She wasn't sure how long she had been sleeping like that, but it hurt. Megan followed Nocturne into the bathroom, and they looked awkwardly at each other as they took care of some necessary business. From there, she stumbled out into the rest of the apartment, which was currently unoccupied. There was a blanket on the couch, but otherwise no sign of Tasha.

Fortunately for Megan's mental state, the door opened a few minutes later, and in walked Tasha, holding a beverage tray.

"Good morning," Tasha said with way too much cheer for this soon after waking. "I thought that you might like coffee!"

"Oh, you are the best!"

"I know." She grinned. "It's been a minute since college, but I think that I remembered your coffee order."

"Did I say the best? I meant to say that you are a goddess."

"I know! But thanks for reminding me. Now mention that to Nocturne, because she thinks that she's the only goddess in residence. Oh, and I got a cinnamon hot chocolate for Sophia."

"Thank you so much. That's very kind of you! Did you sleep on the couch last night?"

"Yeah, I did."

"Oh my god, I'm so sorry! We came in and stole your bed. You should have told me. I'm so sorry!"

"Megan, it's okay. I fall asleep on the couch half the time anyway. Nocturne likes to climb up on me, and then I don't want to disturb her, so we just sleep on the couch."

"So, over thirty and sleeping on the couch with your cat most nights?"

"Don't say it! I am *not* some kind of… what do they call it?"

"Spinster is what they used to say."

"Thanks, grandma! I am not a spinster. I just haven't found a compatible person yet."

"Are you looking?"

"Eh, not really. I work too much, plus I'm in tech, which either intimidates people or bores people, and for some it apparently shatters their fragility and they go into conniptions."

"Oh, that sounds like some fascinating dating stories. Do tell!"

"Oh, no! Not without something much stronger than a latte. Why don't you go wake up Sophia and I'll start on breakfast. I'm usually a yogurt kinda girl, but I'm pretty sure that I have what I need for pancakes."

"Pancakes would be amazing. I mentioned something about you being a goddess, right?"

"Yes, yes you did. I see that Nocturne decided to spend the night with y'all. I hope that she wasn't too much trouble for you. Let me get her highness fed, and then I'll work on breakfast for the three lesser beings in this apartment." Tasha cooed at Nocturne, "Isn't that right, baby? You know that you're always the queen!"

Megan left her friend cooing to an excited cat and padded back into the bedroom. "Sophia, are you awake?"

"Mom! I wasn't awake, but I am now."

"Good morning, sweetheart! Your Aunt Tasha has cinnamon hot chocolate for you, and she's making pancakes for breakfast."

"Can't I sleep a bit longer, Mom?"

"You can go back to sleep after breakfast, I promise. I need to talk to Aunt Tasha for a bit anyway. Just come get breakfast and hot chocolate, okay?"

"Ohhhh. Kayyyyy…"

"Thank you, see you in a minute."

As Megan walked back into the kitchen, Tasha looked up from feeding Nocturne and asked, "Is Sophia up?"

"Yes, but she's not happy about it."

"Hmmm, reminds me of someone else, long ago. History 101, wasn't it? Freshman year…"

"Ugh, don't remind me! That class was so early! *Why*? It was awful."

"And yet, you persevered—with a bit of help from your kind

and wonderful roommate. A roommate who has apparently now been upgraded to goddess."

"Oh, no. I'm not living that down anytime soon, am I?"

"Nope! Goddess Tasha has a lovely ring to it, don't you think?"

"Ugh, where's that coffee?"

They ended up having a lovely breakfast together. Tasha made Sophia some cat-shaped pancakes, which were a big hit. Sophia learned what Nocturne's name meant (a piece of music or art dealing with night, often a romantic night theme). After breakfast, Sophia sat on the couch with her book and a stern maternal warning that she would need to get dressed soon.

While they cleaned up the breakfast dishes, Megan asked Tasha about her plans for the day. Tasha responded, "Well, I need to grab an early lunch, and I volunteer at the cat shelter for a few hours starting at noon. I help with socializing and adoptions. You and Sophia should tag along. I bet she'll love socializing the cats!"

"What does cat socializing involve?"

"It depends. Cats like to sleep a lot, so you may end up with a cat napping in your lap. They also like to play, which is really practicing hunting. We have lots of toys at the shelter, so I usually spend a lot of time entertaining cats with those. Mostly, we're just trying to get them used to having humans around and interacting with us so they'll fit in well with their adopters."

"That sounds like fun! Let's do that."

"Do you have time for some yoga? Are you still teaching?"

Megan sighed. "I tried introducing yoga at school a couple years ago, and some idiot mom decided that I was 'steering the children away from Christ,' so that put an end to that. Not long after that, my yoga classes at the local gym were suddenly empty. So I haven't been teaching yoga for a while, but I still do it at home."

"Did you bring your stuff with you?"

"No, I'm pretty sure that I forgot to pack that."

"That's okay, you can borrow some of my yoga pants. It looks like we're still about the same size. I've got an extra mat, too."

"Thanks, Tasha! That would be great."

An hour later, they sat down after yoga, tired and a bit sweaty, but relaxed. "So," Tasha said. "Do you want to talk about it?"

"Well, you know some of it—how Brad cheated on me while I was pregnant with Sophia, and then we worked things out. Things seemed fine after that. It took awhile to trust him, but I didn't sense any issues. We had disagreements and arguments, but nothing major, you know. He had his job at the bank, and his father made sure that he got promoted quickly. I was teaching social studies and history at the middle school and that was great."

"Uh huh."

"I mean, there were some red flags. During COVID, Brad started spending more time at home on the internet; 'doing his own research,' he said. He tried to talk to me about his 'research,' but I wasn't having anything to do with that nonsense. I don't think he liked that."

"Uh oh… So he went down one of those rabbit holes."

"Yeah, do you think that had something to do with this?"

"Maybe. A lot of good people went to bad places during the pandemic, and you know that I'm not one to ever consider Brad one of the 'good people' in the first place. I always suspected that he didn't like me being your friend…" After an awkward pause, Tasha continued, "And I'm not hearing you defend him on that. Did he say something?"

"No. I mean, yes. I mean, he never said anything back in college or when you were my maid of honor or anything. This past summer, though, I thought about maybe coming to Portland for July 4th as a family trip. When I brought it up, he said that he'd never go to Portland because it was full of commies, jews, and n… uh, he used that word. Oh, and a slur about gay people, too."

"Fuck that guy! You should have left him then!"

"I told him to never use that language at home again, and he said that he wouldn't, but yeah, you're right. It really shook me. I knew that he didn't like gay people, because everyone at church was like that, too. I stopped going a few years back. I found a Sunday morning piano class for Sophia, which is pretty hard to find out there. I'm pretty sure that she hates it, and I'm ashamed about that and ashamed that I didn't say anything, but I felt really alone."

"I'm so sorry, Megan! I know that can be hard, to feel so alone. I know how hard it is to stand up, too. It ain't easy at all. You did the best you could and it sounds like you sheltered Sophia, too."

Tasha stood up to give Megan a hug, and they both cried. "I'm really sorry that I haven't seen you in three years."

"We're making up for that now, aren't we?"

With a laugh, they disentangled themselves. Megan looked at her friend and said, "We both could have done better, and I wish that my marriage wasn't falling apart, but I can't tell you how grateful I am that I'm getting my best friend back."

"Me too! Now go get in the shower and I'll work on lunch. Then we can go love on some cats."

CHAPTER 5
GIMME SHELTER

While Megan showered, Tasha called the volunteer coordinator at the shelter to get approval for Megan and Sophia to join her. There were some hesitations, but Tasha explained that some cat therapy might do her friend some good. She knew that the volunteer coordinator believed strongly in the power of cat therapy, and approval was quickly granted.

Once at the shelter, Tasha explained the most important rule, which was to respect the feelings of any cat that they might socialize. Sophia seemed to grasp the concept quickly, which eased Tasha's one big concern. The shelter had recently released a small litter of kittens from foster care, and Sophia quickly gravitated toward them. It was hard to tell who was having more fun—Sophia, or the kittens.

With Sophia distracted, the two adults focused on socializing the adult cats. Tasha went off to complete an adoption interview with a young couple. When she came back, she found Megan sitting in a chair with a big fluffy creamsicle boy in her lap. She leaned against the doorframe and watched her friend gently rub the blissful orange tabby, whispering softly to him. Eventually, Megan looked up and smiled at her.

"How are you?"

"I'm better. It's hard to feel sad when you have a purring cat in your lap."

"That is so true," Tasha responded as she bent down to scoop up a wandering tuxedo. "Isn't that right, little man? Purring cats make life better, don't they? Don't they?" His feline dignity grossly affronted, the tuxedo quickly slipped from her arms. "Okay, Fred, you don't want to be held. Maybe you'll like a string toy."

"Fred?"

"Fred Astaire. Tuxedo cat. Look, I don't get to name them. Well, sometimes we use a name that I suggested."

"It's cute! I don't think that I'd keep that name, but it's cute."

They watched Fred chase the string toy around for a few minutes. Eventually, he got bored and went to sit under Tasha's chair. Megan took advantage of the break in the action to ask, "How often do you volunteer here?"

"The first and third Saturdays of every month, and the fifth, if the month happens to have five Saturdays. I also cover for people if my schedule is clear."

"That's really sweet that you do this."

"Thank you. It's good for me as well. I enjoy spending time at home with Nocturne, but helping these cats is a good break for me as well, especially after a stressful week at work."

"Yeah, how's that going? Are you still doing… uh, graphic design?"

"I still do some of that. I also work on user interface design for apps. The job is okay, I mean… I like the work, I just hate my boss and the soulless corporate grind. I'd really like to work for myself. I'm good at this, and I feel like I've built a good reputation in the field."

"Why don't you, then?"

"One word… insurance."

"Ugh, I get that."

"Hey, not to change the subject…"

"But, you *are* changing the subject." Megan grinned at her.

"Look, I don't know how long you are planning on staying in Portland, but I want you to stay with me, okay? I know it's a bit cozy in my apartment, but we can make it work."

"Thank you, Tasha! That means the world to me. I… Honestly, right now, I don't know what to do. I don't want to go back to Brad. My parents moved to Florida and couldn't take me in anyway—but I also don't want to cramp your style, either."

"Well, there's not much style to cramp, so that's fine." Tasha smiled. "You're a teacher, and I'm pretty sure that PPS is always short on teachers, so if you decide that you want to stay in Portland, I'm sure that you can get a job there."

"Oh, damn! My job! I need to call my principal and tell her that I'm not coming in on Monday, or maybe ever. She was supportive yesterday when I called out for my last class. She might be the only other person in town who knows that Brad was cheating on me." Megan started to choke up.

"It's alright, Megan. Just keep petting Julius there. Listen to him purr."

"Julius? Oh, because he's orange… I get it."

"Megan, I know that you need to do what's best for you and Sophia, and I'll support you no matter what, but this could be a good opportunity for you to start over. I checked while you were in the shower. The teacher's strike is still going on, but PPS offices are open this week. So, if you want, we could see about getting Sophia enrolled, and also maybe see what you would need to do to be a substitute or something."

"Thank you for doing that, Tasha. Let me think about it."

"Meanwhile, we have another priority to take care of."

"Uh oh, what?"

"That hair! It's time to wash that blonde right out of your hair."

Megan laughed. "You're obsessed!"

"Guilty! That blonde makes you look so Stepford. Your natural red was always gorgeous anyway. I know someone who can help, plus I have a gift card and a coupon."

"You? Your hair looks just like it always has."

"Yeah, so you'd be doing me a favor, getting rid of this gift card and coupon for me."

"How did you end up with a gift card and coupon anyway?"

"I went halfsies on a raffle basket at roller derby a while back and we won."

"I'm sorry… Did you say roller derby? What is roller derby?"

"It's a sport, on roller skates. It's uh… hang on." Tasha whipped out her phone and quickly started typing. "Oh, yeah." She typed a bit more, then looked up and grinned at her friend. "Oh yeah, you and Sophia are in for a treat! Guess what we're doing tomorrow afternoon?"

"Uh, I'm not playing roller derby."

"We're not playing, we're watching. There's a juniors double-header tomorrow. Trust me, you're gonna have a blast!"

"I could tolerate watching softball because I played it, and I always enjoyed watching you play soccer, but I'm not sure that I want to watch a bunch of dudes on roller skates hitting each other."

"That's the thing. It's not dudes. This is primarily a women's sport. It's very open and inclusive. Body positive. It's all the things you're gonna want Sophia to learn. Oh…"

"What?"

"Okay, you might hate me later, because I bet that Sophia might get hooked."

"Tasha…"

"It's cool! You probably won't really hate me. More like that love/hate kinda thing."

"*Tasha…*"

"Trust me, this is going to be the best thing ever."

"And how did you hear about roller derby anyway?"

"Uh, I went on a date a while back. This guy was super excited about seeing hot chicks hitting each other."

"You're not helping your case."

"Well, he was super disappointed. I think that he was

expecting fishnets and fistfights and what we saw instead was this amazing sport played by people who kept their clothes on. Anyway, that was our second date and there was not a third. I did hook-up with one of the skaters another time."

"You hooked up with one of the skaters? But, you said that this was a wo— Oh…"

Tasha looked over at Megan, desperately hoping not to see disgust on her face. "Yeah, I wasn't sure how to bring that up."

Megan's expression stayed pointedly neutral. "Well, some things have definitely changed since college."

"Yeah. I guess you could say that."

Tasha breathed a small sigh of relief as she saw a devilish grin start to form on Megan's face. "Oh no, Tasha! You're not getting away that easily. I want details, girl! I mean, I don't need every detail, but how did this happen?"

Tasha grinned back, glad that her friend seemed fine with this bombshell. "Okay, here goes…"

CHAPTER 6
CINNAMON GIRL

A s the trio clambered into Megan's car, a random thought popped into her mind.

I gotta get HOP cards for me and Sophia.

Yet another item on a list that seemed to get longer every time she thought about it.

Megan was feeling unmoored. Just thirty-six hours ago, life was normal; routine. Then there was Brad's infidelity, the long drive to Portland, reconnecting with her college roommate and (renewed) best friend, and then finding out that Tasha was a lesbian. Okay, maybe not a lesbian—Tasha said that she wasn't calling herself anything right now, because she needed to figure herself out. Anyway, it was a lot for Megan to process in a short amount of time. Unmoored seemed like the perfect word right now.

Priority list. What is important? What do I need to concentrate on and what is noise? Concentrate on what needs to get done. Everything else is noise.

Brad? As unbelievable as it might have seemed, given that they had been married for a decade, he was just noise. Definitely the kind of obnoxious noise that she didn't need right now.

And Tasha's revelations about her sexuality?

Does Tasha's interest in women have any impact on my need to decide to accept her offer? Yes/No? Definitely No. I want to support my friend and, hey, being close by makes being supportive easier. Okay, that sounds like a slight yes, it does have an impact. Spiraling—need to focus.

The big question… *Should I accept Tasha's offer? That means that Sophia and I are staying in Portland for the foreseeable future. Am I okay with that? I think so. More importantly, is this what is best for Sophia? That's the real question.*

From the backseat, Tasha said, "You know, I could get used to this. It's like Driving Ms. Tasha."

Megan laughed, "Oh, I see now. You want us to stay in Portland so that you can have a personal chauffeur."

"You know it!"

"Are we staying here, Mommy?"

"Let's talk about it later, okay, sweetheart? Tasha, when we get back, can you give us some time to talk?"

"Yeah, sure. I'll go ahead and fix some hot chocolate. Sounds good?"

"That would be great, thank you."

The three of them settled into an uncomfortable silence for the next few minutes, until Megan found a free space near Tasha's apartment. Tasha got out, and Megan turned to her daughter.

"Aunt Tasha offered to let us stay with her here in Portland."

"Are we ever going home again?"

"I don't know, sweetheart."

"Why? I miss Daddy."

"I know, Sophia. It's hard to explain. Ummmm… A long time ago, before you were born, your father did something that made me very upset. He promised that he would never do it again, but yesterday I found out that he was doing it again."

"Is Daddy bad because he broke his promise to you?"

"Sweetie, I don't want you to think of your daddy as a bad person. He's made mistakes and he's made Mommy very angry, but you need to make up your own mind about him. I know that's hard, but your feelings need to be your own, not Mommy's. Does that make sense?"

"I think so."

"Right now, though, your Aunt Tasha has offered us a place to stay. What do you think about that?"

"Does that mean that I'll go to a different school?"

"Yes, it does. Are you okay with that?"

"Yeah. The kids at my school can be really mean sometimes."

"Well, I don't know if the kids here would be better, but they would be different. Are you sure that you wouldn't miss your friends?"

"Maybe, but I think I'd be okay. Plus, I like Aunt Tasha a lot!"

"That's good. You haven't seen her since you were five, though."

"That's okay! I like her cat, and she makes you laugh. You and Daddy never laughed. I heard you and Aunt Tasha laughing a lot today. What was so funny?"

Yeah, that's a conversation for a later date, Megan thought to herself. "We were remembering old times and having fun with the cats. Did you have fun with the kittens?"

"Yes! They were so much fun! Can we get one?"

"Not right now, sweetheart, but maybe once we are settled down again we can talk about it. Does that sound good?"

"Yeah, that sounds good. Mommy? Are we going to talk more? Because Aunt Tasha said that she was making hot chocolate. She makes the best hot chocolate!"

"Okay, okay. Wait… Better than my hot chocolate?"

"Yeah! She puts cinnamon in hers."

"Oh, I see now! Well, I guess that I'm going to need to do better, then. Let's go, munchkin, so you can get some of Aunt Tasha's hot chocolate."

"Yay! Race you!"

They raced up the stairs, and Sophia won—not that there was any doubt of the outcome.

As Megan closed the door, Tasha grinned and asked, "Out of breath?"

"Chasing an eight-year-old is great cardio. Who knew? Now, if I could just bottle her energy, then I would make a fortune!"

"I bet." Tasha laughed.

"I have a bone to pick with you," Megan said in a serious voice.

"Uh oh, that sounds ominous."

"Yes, this is very serious. Apparently, you are using cinnamon in hot chocolate as a way to pierce my aura of motherly infallibility."

"What? Girl, that sounds like a 'you' problem!"

"Oh no, girl! Don't you 'girl' me!," Megan shrieked as they both collapsed on the couch laughing.

As she sipped her hot chocolate, Megan tried to remember the last time that she and Brad had laughed about anything. She drew a blank. Whenever the last time was, it was a long time ago. Megan smiled over at her daughter, struck by Sophia's insight.

Turning her head, she whispered, "Hey, Tasha. We do need to talk. We haven't been roommates for a long time, so we'll need to figure out how to live with each other again."

Tasha's face lit up. "Are you saying what I think you're saying?"

"Yes. Sophia and I would like to live with you, at least until we get back on our feet. I'm gonna do my best to make sure that we aren't imposing for too long."

"Megan, you aren't imposing. Well, unless I come home and find a sock on the door…"

"Hey! That was mostly freshman year, and that was because we were in that triple with Lauren!"

"Oh my God, Lauren! I haven't thought of her in forever. I do give her credit for our good grades freshman year."

"Yeah, socks on the door meant that we spent a lot of Friday and Saturday nights in the library."

"Tuesdays and Wednesdays too, for some reason."

"You're right! I totally forgot about that."

"What are you two laughing at?" Sophia asked.

"Nothing!"

"Jinx!"

"Mommy! What's so funny? No fair! You can't tell jokes and not tell me, too…"

Megan and Tasha barely avoided spilling hot chocolate on the couch as they collapsed in a fit of giggles. When Sophia jumped on the couch between them, the tickling started and soon all three were giggling like mad.

CHAPTER 7
THE WILD, WILD LIFE

Tasha watched Megan emerge sleepily from the bedroom, reaching down to rub her legs. "Mornin' sleepyhead! Did Nocturne bother you in the night?"

"Ugh, how are you so cheerful? And, no, Nocturne is fine. She's kinda cute, actually."

"Yes, she is. And don't go stealing my cat's affections!"

"Oh, you mean like how you're stealing my daughter's affections with your cinnamon hot chocolate magic?"

"Exactly! Hey, is Sophia still asleep?"

"Yeah, Nocturne just snuggled up to her and they are both out like a light."

"Cool. You'll never guess what I've been up to."

"Nope."

"I did some cybersleuthing and found Lauren."

"Lauren?"

"Freshman year, socks on the door, Lauren…"

"Oh, right."

"So… she runs an adult boutique in Newark."

"She runs a what?"

"You heard me. Get this, she wants me to do some graphic design work for her website."

"Wow, that's crazy! That's awesome, too. Congrats?"

"I know, right? She's gonna Zoom… Never mind, she's Zooming me now. Hey, Lauren!"

"Hey, yourself, Tasha! Wait… who is that behind you? Is that Megan?"

"Hi, Lauren, it's me."

"Stop, are you two living together? Because freshman year I totally saw the vibe between the two of you—"

"Whoa! Slow down! No, we're not together. Megan's just staying with me for a bit. Nothing like that."

"That's too bad! I always imagined you two together."

"I'm married, Lauren. Well, at least technically."

"I did that twice—it didn't work. I'm in a polyamorous relationship now and it's been great. Hang on… Please tell me that you didn't marry that Brad douche that you were dating in senior year."

"Uh…"

"Ugh, I dated him briefly sophomore year," Lauren said. "Best sleep I got that year, too."

"Wait, what?"

"Boring. I'm saying that he was incredibly boring. In and out of bed, actually."

"Oh, uh… This is a lot right now."

"Sorry. I sometimes overshare. Look, Tasha, I just wanted to catch up real fast. I'll email you some stuff for the website and we can chat. Also, send me your address so I can mail you your check… and I'll send you ladies some samples. After Brad, I know that at least one of you needs them desperately!"

"Lauren!"

"Okay, you two have fun! Definitely do what I would do! Ciao!" Lauren broke the connection with a very suggestive wink.

Tasha let out an embarrassed giggle. "Wow… that was a lot for this early on a Sunday! You okay? Megan?" Tasha waved her hand in front of Megan's face. "Earth to Megan?"

"Holy shit. I'm all for sex positivity, but I think that I might have needed coffee before that." Megan's face was beet red.

Tasha snickered. "I bet you're awake now, though."

"Yeah, no doubt. Was Lauren serious about sending us some samples?"

"I'm pretty sure she was. Let's just make sure that your girl doesn't open that particular toybox!"

"Stop! You're terrible." Megan laughed.

"Yep, and you love me for it."

"I do. Now, since I'm fully awake with no need for coffee, do you want me to start on breakfast?"

"I'm actually running a bit low on stuff. Could I ask you a big favor, roomie?"

"Sure… roomie. Let me guess, grocery run? Is the store even open?"

"It's not that early and we're in the city. It's open. I have a list on the fridge. If you don't mind doing that and maybe even making breakfast when you get back," Tasha batted her eyelashes at her friend.

"Of course, I'd be happy to. Let me put on real pants, though."

"Good thinking! Meanwhile, I have a ton of work to get through this morning so that Kevin doesn't murder me when I walk in on Monday. He still might, just because he's a jerk, but less likely if I knock out a couple of client projects."

"Kevin really does sound lovely… I'm looking forward to meeting him if your company has an office holiday party. Kidding!"

"Oh, you think that you're gonna get an invite to the holiday party, do you? Only if you're really nice to me." Tasha paused, tapping her lips with her forefinger. "Oh, actually, that could be kinda fun. It's usually awful, and if you come as my plus one, that will really throw Kevin for a loop. I might actually enjoy the party for once. Great idea, Megan."

"Uh, thanks? Okay, I'm off as soon as I get pants on. See you back here soon."

Tasha threw herself into work for the next few hours. She worried that having Megan and Sophia in the apartment would be distracting, but, weirdly, it felt pretty good. Sophia kept Nocturne distracted, which actually made working at home easier, since she no longer had a cat "helping" her work. Tasha closed her laptop around eleven and stretched. She watched Sophia playing with one of Nocturne's feather toys, and it was hard to say who was having more fun.

Tasha poked her head into the bedroom to find Megan reading on the bed. "Whatcha reading?"

"Uh, *Lamb* by Christopher Moore."

"Oh yeah, I liked that one. What do you think?"

"It's fun. I'm not too far into it. Brad would hate it, which kinda makes me like it even more. That's not weird, is it?"

"Nope! I might have to re-read after you're done. Feel free to read any of my books. We can get you set up with a library card, too. It's pretty easy, and Multnomah County has a really good public library system. Hey, are you and Sophia good for burgers on the way to roller derby?"

"Sure! Burgers sound great. Do we need to go soon?"

"Yeah, in five or ten minutes," Tasha said. An alert popped up on her phone. She smiled wryly. "Well, I just got an alert that a delivery pick-up has been scheduled for a package shipping from Newark, New Jersey tomorrow."

"Oh my god, Lauren was actually serious."

"Apparently she was. Tell you what, when it gets here, I'll take Sophia out for a movie or something. I'll have some bonding time with my goddaughter and you can um, take care of some personal needs."

Tasha barely avoided the pillow that rocketed toward her head, laughing as she ducked back into the living area. "Hey, Sophia! Your Mom is gonna need you to put on your shoes and coat, and then I've got a special surprise for you this afternoon."

"Okay! I like surprises!"

She turned as Megan walked out of the bedroom and whispered, "You might want to throw a bit of water on your face. You look a bit flushed." Tasha grinned wickedly at Megan. "Ow! No need for punching. I'm just trying to look out for my best friend and this is the thanks I get. I wonder if I need to pick up batteries this week…" The look on Megan's face was priceless.

"Oh, look, Lauren just texted me," Tasha said, turning her phone screen toward Megan. "Tell Megan to lose the blonde hair. That's definitely my color, not hers."

Megan sighed in exasperation. "Seriously?"

Tasha laughed all the way to the car.

CHAPTER 8
PUSH IT!

"So, how come you don't have a car, Tasha?"

"Eh, Portland is super easy to get around in by public transit. If I need something more than that, well then there's rideshares or rentals. Honestly, derby is one of the few places that isn't easily accessible by transit, which is a pain. It's a lot of fun, though, so it's worth it."

Megan pondered this while they waited for their burgers. "I dunno, I'm really used to driving everywhere."

"That's okay, especially for now. Figure things out, and then decide about the car."

"You're right. Now, tell us a bit about what we're about to… oh, damn! Those are some good-looking burgers." The burgers were meaty and loaded with bacon, paired with freshly-cut fries.

Conversation ceased for a few minutes as the trio dug into their lunch. After a bit, Megan tried to listen as Tasha explained what she knew about roller derby, but she wasn't getting it. "Okay, I think that maybe it will help if I just see it."

"Yeah, that helped for me. And then when I had questions, I just asked the people next to me."

"Really? Isn't that weird?"

"Usually I'd say yes, but derby is pretty chill. You'll see."

"Wow… If we do this again, then we're coming back here."

"Definitely. Are you ready to head out?"

It only took a few minutes to get to the Hangar, although Megan was glad to have Tasha's guidance. They parked in the lot and made their way to the big metal building. "I see why they call it the Hangar," Megan said.

As they entered, they watched kids in blue and red uniforms skating around an oval track in the middle of the floor. Megan thought that they looked pretty small. "You said juniors. How old are these kids?"

"The Rose Petals are seven to twelve years old, I think. The next game is the Rose Buds, and they're twelve to seventeen or something like that."

"Look, Sophia. They're your age."

"I know! That's so cool!"

"Okay, now I understand why you told me that I might hate you after this."

Tasha snickered in response.

They found seats on the bleachers and settled in, watching the two teams warm up and listening to the crowd around them. The Hangar was a large open space with seating around the track in the middle and two team benches on the far side.

Megan relaxed enough to strike up a conversation with the people around her. The crowd was mostly the family of skaters, and they were all friendly and welcoming. She looked over and saw Tasha smile at her and she returned the smile. After about twenty minutes, Tasha leaned over and pointed to the far side between the team benches. "Do you see that guy in the sequined jacket over there with the referees? He's the emcee, which means that the game is about to start."

Megan found herself enjoying the game, even if she wasn't always sure what was going on. The skaters with stars on their helmets were jammers who scored points by passing opposing blockers. There was a blocker with a striped helmet, and they could take the jammer's star. One thing was for sure—it was fun and fast-paced, especially the second game with the older kids. Their increased size, experience, and athleticism made the game even faster. Megan especially enjoyed Sophia's delight when a jammer defied gravity, leaping across the apex of the oval track to bypass the entire pack of blockers.

As they walked out a couple hours later, Megan watched her daughter practically bouncing off the walls. "You know this is all your fault, right?" she said to Tasha.

"Yep."

"You created this monster, and now I have to live with her."

"Correction, now we both have to live with her."

"True… Thank you, Tasha. This was a lot of fun, and clearly Sophia enjoyed it as well. I think that we both needed this."

"I'm not surprised. This really is a great community. They even have a recreational league. I'd totally join if I thought that my knee would hold up."

"Still bothering you?"

"Yeah, it still aches when a thunderstorm is coming. Although one nice benefit to Portland is that we don't get many thunderstorms."

"Mommy, Mommy! Can I do that? I have my own skates!"

"Let's see about that, okay? And I think that you might need new skates."

"You're the best!"

Tasha smiled. "What about your Aunt Tasha? Remember, this was my surprise, and I will make you cinnamon hot chocolate."

"Aunt Tasha is the best!"

"Hey now."

Tasha wrapped an arm around Megan's shoulders. "We can both be the best, it's not a competition!"

"Says the woman trying to steal my daughter's affection."

"Do or do not, there is no try."

For a weekend that started in tears, Megan couldn't remember that last time she had laughed this much. She knew that there were difficult times ahead, but she felt a lot better about facing the future.

"You win. I'll ditch the blonde."

"*Yes!*"

CHAPTER 9

MANIC MONDAY

Monday morning was a shitshow—a productive shitshow, but a shitshow nonetheless.

Megan and Sophia walked less than five minutes to get to the closest school. There were certainly benefits to enrolling a new student mid-semester during the third week of a teacher's strike. The office staff was really bored and all caught up on paperwork. They were also incredibly grateful to see a new face, which made navigating the bureaucratic red tape easier, but it was still a process. By the end of the day, Sophia was successfully registered, and Megan had filled out the necessary paperwork to be a substitute teacher whenever the strike ended.

She was certain that none of this truly required a personal meeting with the principal and vice-principal, but she suspected that they were happy to see new faces and fill some time in a very open schedule.

Sophia seemed excited about her new school, which eased Megan's anxiety. Things were looking up when they stopped at the nearest library. Registering with the Multnomah County Public Library system was refreshingly easy after a morning with Portland Public Schools. They returned to Tasha's apartment—home, at least for now—with some new books to read. She fixed a light lunch for Sophia and herself. After lunch, Sophia went to read on the couch, where a very pleased Nocturne hopped up to occupy Sophia's lap. Megan was just starting to do some job searches to see if there were opportunities for a part-time yoga instructor when her phone rang. Her heart sank when she saw the name on the screen… Brad.

"Sophia, keep reading, sweetie. Mommy's going to go for a walk."

"Okay!"

Megan steeled herself as she fast-walked to the door, grabbing a coat on the way. She swiped the phone screen as she closed the door. "What is it, Brad?" she said angrily.

"What is it? You run away from home, you take *my* daughter, and you don't bother to call for three damn days, and *that's* how you answer my call?"

"First, she's our daughter. Second, I wasn't the one caught with my dick inside my secretary, so I'll answer the phone however I want."

"She wasn't my secretary!"

"Not helping yourself, dumbass."

"It's like I told you on Friday, it didn't mean anything."

"Our marriage or your affair?"

"Our mar— I mean, the affair! I love you, not her."

"Yeah, you said that on Friday, too, and I'm guessing that she didn't agree with that. What was her name, Margaret?"

"Uh…."

"Let me guess. You spent the weekend trying to make up for that particular fuck-up with Margaret, and when that didn't work out, now you're calling me. Am I right?"

"No, it's not like that! I was just giving you some space. I love you, Megan."

"You have a strange way of showing it then."

"I made a mistake! I've been under a lot of pressure at work and I wasn't thinking straight. I don't even know what I saw in her."

"Her name is Margaret. You introduced me to her and her husband at the holiday party last year," Megan said with painfully deliberate sweetness. "And I know damn well what you saw in her, because I saw all of her, too. And I mean all of her."

"I, uh…"

"Shut up, Brad. Thank you for that, by the way. Now I don't have to wonder what she does or doesn't have compared to me. She definitely has bigger tits, and I'm never going bald down there. Do you like that hairless look? I haven't been hairless down there since puberty. Wait, is that what you like?"

"No, uh…"

"Holy shit, I can hear your brain trying to catch up from here. How long, Brad?" There was silence on the phone for a few seconds.

"Now look, Megan. I just heard about Sophia transferring to a school in Portland. I can't believe you took her to that God-forsaken Gomorrah! Are you living on the streets?"

Megan was unsurprised by Brad's sudden aggressive questioning. She knew that he hated being out of control, and he was showing her just how much she had thrown him. She forced a pleasant tone into her voice as she responded, "Oh, it's been very nice, actually. The local communist party welcomed us in. We're in a tent commune right now. All the drugs you can take, and every weekend they throw gay orgies."

"You're going to b—"

Megan hung up before Brad even finished. As much as she enjoyed messing with his head, she knew that at some point they were going to have to try to hold a mature discussion about Sophia's future as well as their own. Clearly, Brad was not ready for that, and if she was being honest with herself, she wasn't either. This was all still too raw right now.

Megan leaned back against the door to Tasha's apartment as she did breathing exercises to clear her head and settle herself down. The past two days had been wonderful, and Monday was proving to be an unpleasant return to reality.

I really hate being the person having a personal phone conversation in a hallway. Thankfully, no one was here to witness it.

As she stared at the door to Tasha's apartment, Megan dried off the remnants of her tears and entered. She found Sophia and Nocturne curled up on the couch together, like a child doughnut with cat filling. Sophia didn't bother to look up from her book. The only acknowledgement of Megan's return was Nocturne lazily raising her head, glaring at Megan, and then returning to her nap.

"We need to go to the grocery store. Do you want anything?"

"Ice cream." Sophia's nose was still down in her book.

"Ice cream, what?"

"Chocolate ice cream." She didn't even look up.

"Ice cream, please?"

"Sorry, Mommy. Chocolate ice cream. *Please.*" Sophia finally looked up and smiled.

Megan smiled back. "Alright, let's get your coat. We'll be back soon and you can go back to your reading."

"But Mommy, I'm so comfortable." And with that, Sophia's head was back in her book.

Megan couldn't be upset that her daughter enjoyed reading.

"Alright, fifteen minutes and then we're going. Your Aunt Tasha is being very nice, letting us stay here with her and we're going to make her a nice dinner tonight as a thank you. And we'll get you your ice cream."

CHAPTER 10
9 TO 5

Tasha's day sucked. Kevin was in a mood when she got in. She was glad that she'd done some work on Sunday, even though she resented working on the weekend. If not, her day would have been much worse. As it was, she was called into Kevin's office about leaving early on Friday. Tasha wasn't sure why he bothered to ask since he didn't want to listen to her answer.

Dealing with pig-headed idiots who were somehow in charge despite their clear incompetence was a skill that Tasha had spent years honing. As a woman in the tech world, she had plenty of practice. She liked to think of it as extra credit. That didn't make it better, and it certainly didn't make it more fair, but Tasha had always been good at extra credit.

So, when Kevin dumped a new client on her, Tasha just plugged in her headphones and got to work. She felt the need for something old school, starting off with Grandmaster Flash and Run DMC, moving to Destiny's Child and then a bit of Roxette to mix things up. Megan had introduced her to Roxette back in college, and so Tasha continued down that road with some late-80s Heart and then jumped forward a few decades for The Warning. By mid-afternoon, she was deep in the groove and had finished the client's project—not that she was going to tell Kevin that.

Instead, Tasha started to map out what she was going to do for Lauren's adult boutique website. Doing some freelance work felt exciting, and, since it was for Lauren, it made sense to listen to Mötley Crüe. That girl loved Mötley Crüe, especially when there was a sock on the doorknob. It seemed appropriate.

Tasha left work late, like always. Early on, Kevin had told her, "If you leave on time, it shows that you aren't dedicated. Dedicated people stay late." It was as stupid as just about everything else that Kevin believed, but, like a good little drone, Tasha stayed late. Usually she hated every minute of it, but today she worked on her freelance gig for Lauren, then sent Kevin the finished client project before she left. Let the idiot think that it took her all day.

She took a quick detour over to Powell's Books. Powell's was a dangerous place for a book lover, but Tasha was focused. She kept her head down and actually managed to get out in twenty minutes, which was a new record.

As Tasha walked down the hall to her apartment, she savored the spicy smell coming from one of the apartments. Then, as she opened the door, she realized that the smell was coming from *her* apartment. Surveying the room, she saw Sophia and Nocturne settled on the couch, and Megan in the kitchenette doing something on the stove. Megan quickly turned her head and smiled before turning back. Tasha put her bags down and glided up behind Megan, wrapping her arms around her friend's waist. She propped her chin on Megan's left shoulder and peered over to gaze at the reddish-brown something that Megan was stirring. "Whatcha makin'?" she asked in an extended drawl.

"I thought I'd make some chana masala for dinner. The rice and spinach are done, and I have some naan warming in the oven."

"You are *amazing*! I could totally get used to this. Oh, you smell good, too. Spices and lavender are a good combination."

Megan laughed. "Oh, good—if this teaching thing doesn't

work out I can go into fragrances. Sophia? Sweetie, can you set the table? Megan craned her head, trying to hear Sophia's response. … "What? … Okay, thank you!" Megan whispered, "I have no idea what she said, but she's moving, so that's good. Now go get settled, dinner's almost done."

"Wow, you really are a mom! Thank you for dinner. I'll be ready in a minute. Sophia, look what I picked up for you."

"What is it, Aunt Tasha?"

"I got you this book. It's called *Rollergirl.*"

"Oh, thank you, Aunt Tasha!"

"I hope that you like it."

"Sophia, put your new book down and set the table."

"Yes, Mom," Sophia extended the words into a long whine.

Tasha chuckled as she went to wash up. Coming home like this felt good.

Megan was getting the food on the table as Tasha emerged from the bathroom. Once everything was set, the three of them sat down.

"This is really good, Megan!"

"Thank you. I really like trying new foods from around the world. I haven't had the chance to do it as much as I want to—"

"Because of…"

"Yeah, not the adventurous type. Especially if it involved spices."

"I can't imagine life without spices."

"Me neither." Megan looked Tasha up and down. "Hey, on a totally different topic. I like your skirt and boots. Do you always dress so elegantly for work?"

"You have no idea… Business casual, right? What the hell is business casual anyway? I mean, it's Portland, so definitely not a suit. People look at you funny if you're in a suit. You might as well have a huge sign over your head that says lawyer. It's easy for guys. They wear jeans and a T-shirt and keep a polo in their cubicle in case someone important rolls in. Me, though? Jeans work, but I've never been a jeans girl."

"Yeah, even in college. Every once in a while I saw you in jeans."

"Yeah, every once in a while. Sweatpants are too casual, leggings are… let's just say that the leggings have to go with a skirt. And skirts… One time I wore a red skirt, kinda mid-length, it wasn't even a mini, with stockings and knee-high boots." Tasha's voice dropped into a whisper. "Holy shit, I shut the company down that day. It was so bad that Kevin's boss came down. Imagine some middle-aged middle manager trying to ask me to never wear that outfit again without actually saying that. After that, I only wear knee-length skirts or longer. I'm still not sure if I should be mad about being objectified or giddy because every guy in the place had to pick his tongue off the floor. Maybe both?"

"That's kinda gross, but kinda empowering, too, in a weird way. I get you, though. I had a few dads give me the full-body-scan at parent-teacher conferences."

"*Gross*! You're married, and a mom, and their kids' teacher. That ain't right."

"Ugh, it was even worse if the wife was there."

"So creepy…"

"So… is that why you swore off men?"

"Uh, I haven't sworn off men. I'm just trying to explore who I am and what I like. Who do I connect with best? Like, I've connected before, but it was never like a *deep* connection, you know?"

"You mean love?"

"Yeah. Like, I've been in love, but I don't know if it was ever the real thing."

"I hear you. After the past few days, I am certain that I'm in the same boat. Well, except for Sophia. She's my everything, especially now."

Sensing that this might be dangerous territory for Megan, Tasha steered the conversation back to more mundane subjects. She suspected that her friend needed to talk about this, but probably not at the dinner table with her daughter. Thankfully, Sophia had been too busy eating and scratching Nocturne, and she'd hopefully missed that last bit of conversation. Tasha reached over, squeezed Megan's hand, and gave her a quick smile. Megan smiled back.

"After dinner, can you show us how to feed Nocturne? Sophia and I should know how to do it, just in case you're running late."

"Sure thing! Thank you. Oh, and speaking of running late, let me tell you about Kevin's thoughts on working late."

"Oh no…"

CHAPTER 11
TELEPHONE

Tuesday was a day for more errands. Megan set up an account at a local credit union and applied for a credit card. It was definitely time to untangle her finances from Brad's. After she finished that major priority, she started checking off a host of lesser priorities. She was feeling pretty good about the day when her phone buzzed. A new text.

Brad: You need to come home before I press charges for kidnapping my daughter

Megan: I didn't kidnap our daughter. I took her to safety

Brad: 🐄💩

Megan: Just stop

We need to have a mature conversation About us

About Sophia

Brad: Then come home and we can talk

Megan: That is not the answer. I'm not in a good place to have that conversation and you aren't either

Brad: Then when

Megan: I don't know. Maybe Saturday. Maybe we'll have cooled down by then.

Brad: 😕

Stop stealing my money

Megan: Fucking hell Brad

It's a JOINT account. That's my money in there too Now you're just pissing me off again

If you ever want to have a real conversation then you need to back the fuck off

Brad: Fine

Megan let him have the last word, because she knew that he would drag this on. She felt like she had two children in her life, and Sophia was the more mature one. Her phone buzzed again with a new text. *What now?*

Tasha: Hey, girl

Megan: Glad its you Brad just texted me

Tasha: What did that shithead want

Megan: The usual

Tasha: Is his head still stuck in his ass

Megan: Like I said The usual

Tasha: LOL

I need to ask you something

Megan: Sure what

Tasha: Okay the hair place had a cancelation
tomorrow so I got you in at 3. Can you make it

Megan: LOL Thanks I think I can make it by 3

Tasha: Awesome You said that you wanted to get
rid of the blonde

Megan: And you said that I should go with wild
colors

Tasha: YES get wild

Megan: Which color should I get

Tasha: Green would fit the Irish thing Hot pink
would be super sexy

Purple would be sexy too, subtle sexy

Megan: Didn't you mention fire truck red

Tasha: I did but your natural red is better

Megan: You've thought a lot about this

Tasha: IKR Another question

I was going to this Friendsgiving at my friend
Maria's Wanna come

Sophia is welcome too

Megan: So you already asked Maria

Tasha: Yeah she said the more the merrier

Megan: What kind of friend should I be jealous

The conversation paused there. After a minute, Megan started to get worried that she had said the wrong thing and upset Tasha.

Megan: Kidding!!!!!

After even more time passed, Tasha finally replied.

Tasha: About that. Full disclosure Maria and I
dated briefly

Megan: Ok

Tasha: It was a couple years ago and we are
friends now

Megan: DETAILS

There was another pause.

Tasha: Fuller disclosure it was at the end of 2020
We met at a singles mixer

I was looking for a holiday date but the guys
there sucked We started chatting and hit it off

Megan: So what happened

Tasha: We went out a few times We decided we
were better friends

Megan: No connection?

Tasha: Yeah No connection

Megan: Even though there was no connection
Was there still a CONNECTION

Tasha: OMFG UR terrible

Megan: You still love me though

Another pause.

Tasha: Yes, I love you. Ok Fullest disclosure We
slept together

Megan: Did she punch your Lesbian V Card

Tasha: That's not a thing And yes

Megan: Did you break up because the sex
was bad

Tasha: OMFG UR the worst No it was amazing

Megan: Did she break up with you because you
were bad at girl sex

Tasha: I have never had any complaints Including
from Maria

We had a spark but not a fire

Megan: I get that Thank you for telling me Yes to
friendsgiving

Tasha: Great

Now that UR done grilling me about girl sex start
thinking of something to bring Maria will have
turkey and tofurkey plus stuffing and mashed
potatoes Everything else is potluck

Megan: Cool

Tasha: I have to get back to work Have any
music recommendations

Megan: Hang on

Check out The Sounds

I think you will like them

Tasha: Thanks

CU2nite

After recommending The Sounds to Tasha, she decided to listen to them as well. Megan put her headphones on and fired up their first album. As "Dance With Me" started playing, she checked to see when her bus was coming. Pretty soon. Tasha was right about Portland being fairly easy to get around on transit. She relaxed and immersed herself in the beat.

CHAPTER 12

GIRLS JUST WANNA HAVE FUN

The Wednesday before Thanksgiving was usually a relatively easy day for Tasha.

Clients were generally already on holiday and Kevin was just assigning busywork. She had a couple of big client projects going on, but she had those mostly handled at this point and was waiting for the clients to get back next week. Plus, she had finished that freelance work for Lauren the night before. Lauren was ecstatic about the new website design. Speaking of Lauren, Tasha received a delivery alert on her phone. Apparently that "sample basket" was arriving today in the late afternoon.

Tasha grinned devilishly and called Megan. "Hey, Tasha! What's up?" Megan asked.

"Kevin caught an early flight, so it's really quiet here."

"What about 'being dedicated to the company' and stuff?"

Tasha laughed bitterly. "That only applies to us worker drones, not to Kevin."

"Of course…"

"Hey, so I was thinking. Why don't you drop Sophia off here with me? Then you can go down to Dye Dye My Darling to get your hair done, and I'll have some 'girl time' with Sophia."

"Are you sure that's okay?"

"Yeah, totally. Kevin's not here and there's plenty for her to do. We're one of those 'fun offices' with video games and ping pong."

"Oh, that sounds nice!"

"Trust me, it isn't. Anything that might be relaxing or fun means that you aren't showing dedication and we all know how Kevin feels about that."

"That guy is such an asshole!"

"He really is the worst."

"Okay, sounds like fun. I'll bring Sophia over after lunch."

Tasha enjoyed her afternoon with Sophia, especially getting to show her how graphic design worked. Sophia showed some artistic flair, and Tasha enjoyed watching her get engrossed in using the design tools to create pictures. They stayed until 4:56pm, because of course Kevin sent a Slack message at 4:55pm about something trivial, clearly checking to see if Tasha was still there. Goddess, she hated his stupid games.

Tasha grabbed the delivery from the mailroom when they got home. Sophia asked, "What's that, Aunt Tasha?"

"Nothing, sweetie. Just some food for Nocturne that I ordered." There was no way that Tasha was going to explain what was almost certainly a box full of sex toys to an eight-year-old. If Megan wanted to, that was totally up to her, and Tasha would be happy to observe that conversation.

"Did you have fun today?"

"Yes! I liked your computer games. Is that what you do all day?"

"Well, it's a bit more complex and not always as fun for me, but yes."

"That's really cool! Maybe I should do that when I grow up."

"I bet that you can do anything when you're grown up! I've got an idea. How about we have a girls night, just you me. I'll make us some mac and cheese, and then we can go roller skating. Does that sound good?"

"That sounds fun, Aunt Tasha! What about Mommy?"

"Your mom has had a lot going on lately. I think that she might like some time to do mom things. Think of this as a present to her."

"Okay, I like making Mommy happy!" Sophia paused. "Aunt Tasha, you make Mommy happy. She laughs a lot with you."

"Thank you, Sophia! That's very kind of you to say."

Tasha made them dinner, fed Nocturne, and then started working on a surprise for Megan. She opened the box from Lauren and gave a soft whistle. Lauren had been *very* generous. There were quite a few interesting objects in the box, some of which Tasha had never seen before, and the quality of the contents was really good. She would definitely have to send Lauren a very nice thank you. Once Megan texted with her estimated return time, Tasha set her plan into motion.

As Megan was walking in, Tasha was bundling Sophia out the door. "Sophia and I are going to have a 'girls night' tonight! We're going roller skating. I have dinner for you on the stove, there's wine in the fridge, and I drew a nice hot bath for you. Oh… and Lauren's care package arrived today. It's in the top of the closet. *Have fun!*" Tasha scampered out the door with the image of Megan's shocked face dancing in her brain. She laughed as she took Sophia's hand. It would be an enjoyable night for all three of them, in very different ways.

CHAPTER 13
JOYRIDE

Megan woke up on Thursday feeling better than she had in a while. She definitely owed Lauren a very nice thank you. She was really grateful that Tasha had texted her last night to say when she and Sophia would be back. That gave her time to set up her own surprise for Tasha—an air mattress for Megan and Sophia to sleep on. Megan felt more than a bit guilty about stealing Tasha's bed. Tasha insisted that she slept on the couch a lot of nights anyway, but Megan didn't want her to feel like she had to sleep on the couch in her own apartment.

Looking over, she saw that Sophia was still asleep, so she quietly got up and started working on breakfast and coffee. Not long after, she heard Tasha waking up. A couple minutes later, Tasha padded into the kitchenette to join her.

Megan whispered, "Good morning, Tasha. How did you sleep?"

"I slept well. I really don't mind the couch, but thank you. You're very sweet. You're also still glowing, and I bet that it's not because of the air mattress..."

Megan blushed. She reached out and embraced her friend. Not a quick hug, but one of those comfort hugs where you just sort of melt into each other and feel the joy of connecting with another person. A body and soul hug.

"Thank you, Tasha. I didn't realize how much I needed last night."

"I've got you, Megan. Any time you need that again, you tell me, okay?"

"Same for you. I don't want to cramp your style."

As they released their hug, Megan turned her head to give Tasha a friendly kiss on the cheek. Tasha apparently had the same idea because both of their heads turned at the same time and they ended up with a quick kiss on the lips instead.

"Oh, I'm so sorry!" Megan exclaimed as she once again blushed furiously. "I meant to kiss you on the cheek."

"Same! I'm sorry, too!"

They looked at each other awkwardly. "Um, I'm going to make a quick trip to the store after I eat. I hate being a Thanksgiving shopper, but I thought that Sophia and I could make cupcakes for Friendsgiving today. Do you need anything?"

"That's great. Let me see what supplies I have for cupcakes. I think I'm gonna whip up my famous chili mac. I'll make a list of what I need."

"Sounds good, Tasha. Let me finish my yogurt and put on some real pants. Speaking of—what's the dress code for today?"

"Whatever you want to wear is fine. Some people will be in jeans, and some go all-out. I like to dress up a bit for this. Just because I don't get too many other opportunities to get dolled up. Feel free to look in my closet if you wanna borrow something."

The three of them spent the morning in and out of the kitchen. Megan decided to do the cupcakes from scratch. It wasn't much harder than a box and people were always impressed. Plus, it would be fun to show Sophia some real baking. Tasha kept the stovetop occupied with her chili, but that was an off-and-on process, so her cooking didn't interfere with their baking.

Megan and Sophia were done with the oven before Tasha started on the mac and cheese. Megan watched as Tasha walked

Sophia through the steps of how to make her homemade mac and cheese, and the two of them combined it with the chili to create Tasha's fabled chili mac. Then Sophia got a lesson in how to make homemade buttercream frosting. Knowing her daughter, Megan made extra—Sophia was definitely going to sneak some frosting. Tasha helped out with that while her chili mac baked.

The trio had a light lunch, then got ready for Friendsgiving. Megan and Tasha went through the latter's closet, looking for something to wear. Megan's limited supply of dressy items were hundreds of miles away, but thankfully she and Tasha were about the same size. Tasha insisted that she try on a long purple dress with a scandalously high side-slit. She said that it would match Megan's new hair color. Checking herself in the bathroom mirror, Megan had to agree. Her hair was now a purple so dark that it was nearly black, with lavender highlights, and it matched well with the rich purple of the dress. Strappy black wedge sandals completed the look. She exited the bathroom, feeling both giddy and a bit self-conscious about just how much of her leg showed as she walked.

Megan and Tasha saw each other simultaneously, each struck speechless by the other.

Tasha recovered first, exclaiming, "Damn, girl! I thought I looked good in that dress, but wow, you wear it well!"

As Megan looked at Tasha in her shimmering red minidress, she realized that she hadn't seen Tasha wearing anything except pants and sleeved shirts in the past week. She realized this because she was absolutely sure that she would have remembered seeing those tattoos— what appeared to be a panther stalking out of a ruined jungle temple on Tasha's right thigh, and a band of thorns wrapping around her right arm. Cat pawprints trailed up Tasha's left arm and disappeared under the top of the dress.

"Wow, that dress looks amazing on you! And you never told me that you have tattoos."

"I... um... I'm deliberate about when I show them off, and where. I love them, but there is a lot of pain attached."

"I bet! That leg one looks like it took forever."

"Well, that did hurt a lot. No, I mean… I got the thorns back when I was still living in Charleston. Momma saw it and told me it was sacrilegious to have Jesus' crown of thorns tattooed on my arm."

"Oh, no…"

"Yeah… and then I told her that it wasn't about Jesus and that I didn't care anyway because I was an atheist."

"Oh, shit…"

"We haven't spoken since. Six months later, I took a job here."

"Oh, Tasha! I'm so sorry."

"It's okay, really."

Somehow, Megan didn't believe that. She heard the strain behind Tasha's apparent cheer. Now wasn't the time to talk about it, though.

Shifting the conversation, Megan asked, "Did you have that panther tattoo the day that you shut your office down by wearing a skirt?"

Tasha laughed. "No, I got the panther after that incident. I actually bought the dress that you're wearing after I got this done. The side slit shows glimpses of the tattoo as I walk." She smiled. "I definitely turn some heads with that! Oh, maybe since you look so good in that dress, you should get something similar on your leg."

"Um, I don't have any tattoos. I think that might be a bit much, especially for my first time."

"Don't you worry, I'll get you inked up yet!"

"Um…"

"Come on now, let's go celebrate."

They exited the bedroom, and a wonderstruck Sophia gasped. "Mommy! You're so pretty!"

"Thank you, sweetheart."

"Aunt Tasha! Your tattoos are so cool!"

Tasha grinned at Megan and mouthed, "Your turn."

Megan rolled her eyes and grabbed the cupcakes.

CHAPTER 14

CAN'T TAKE MY EYES OFF OF YOU

They could hear music playing as they walked up to Maria's door. Tasha had never actually described Maria, so Megan had filled in a mental image of a badass woman who wore leather jackets or tailored suits. Those images completely crumbled as a woman in jeans and an absolutely hideous Christmas sweater gleefully embraced Tasha.

"You must be Sophia and Megan! I'm Maria. Come on in!"

There were hugs all around as Maria took their coats and directed them to the food. There were too many people for formal dining, so there were people scattered about, which made introductions challenging. Megan appreciated the warm welcome, but was very glad to see how welcoming everyone was of Sophia. Her daughter was the only non-adult, but everyone was very kind and made sure to include her. Seeing this helped Megan relax as she mingled with the other guests, but she always kept an eye out. She noted that Tasha also seemed to keep a permanent eye on Sophia as well.

Afternoon turned to evening in a flurry of eating and conversation. The other guests were a fascinating array of people, all of whom seemed to have some connection to Maria. After spending most of the last decade with other moms, Megan felt a bit out of her element.

Whenever she felt her anxiety rising, Tasha seemed to magically appear with some anecdote that kept the conversation moving, and a light touch on Megan's arm that soothed her anxiety.

The energy of the Friendsgiving celebration mellowed as the evening stretched out and people started drifting off to other events. Megan found herself leaning against a bookcase with sparkling water in one hand and a brownie in the other. She smiled as she watched Tasha and Sophia join a young couple at a low table to learn a game called Settlers of Catan. Megan grinned as Tasha carefully maneuvered herself into a sitting position while managing not to flash the entire party. *It really is a lovely dress,* Megan mused, *but definitely not practical for some things.* She immediately became conscious of just how much of her own right leg was showing and started fidgeting with her dress.

"You're good for her, you know."

Startled, Megan looked left to see Maria glide up to her. "I, uh… it's not like that."

"I know. She's helping out her old friend. She told me a bit about you. About your situation."

"Um…"

"Not the details of course. Tasha isn't a gossip, but she is a good friend."

"The best."

"I meant what I said, though. Look at her there with your little Sophia. I've never seen Tasha this happy or this comfortable."

"Really? Um, thank you."

"Of course! I've only known Tasha for a handful of years, but I've come to love her… Not that sort of love—we never had that. She told you about us, I presume."

"She did."

"That's good. It's not healthy to have secrets between loved ones."

"We're not…"

Maria gave her a skeptical look. "Love takes many forms. She clearly loves you. And your little girl."

"I guess I wasn't thinking of it that way."

Maria smiled wickedly as she said, "And if you did think of it that way, then I'm sure that Tasha would make it *very* enjoyable."

Megan's face turned a deep scarlet as she took a drink, trying desperately to think of a response.

Maria continued, "I'm only teasing you. Seriously, though, would you care for some unsolicited advice?"

"Um, yes."

"You have many decisions in front of you. Remember that family isn't only blood, it's who you choose to share your life with. It's not my business how your relationship with Tasha is defined. It isn't anyone's business. But she's a person worth keeping in your life, in whatever form that takes. I hope that she keeps you in her life, because her light shines brighter when you are near."

"Thank you, Maria. I'll think about that."

"Good. Now, about the decisions in your life. That's up to you to do what you feel is best for yourself and Sophia. I don't like to talk about dark subjects at an event like this, but if you would like to talk another day, then here's my card. I like to think of myself as a friendly host, but in my day job I'm a divorce lawyer, and I'm a hard-assed bitch when I need to be."

Maria left to tend to other guests, leaving Megan staring at her business card. She wasn't sure if she was ready for that step. After finishing the brownie, she put the card in her purse and went back to watching Tasha and Sophia learn the new game. They both seemed to be having a good time, and Megan smiled as she took it all in. Unconsciously, her hand came up to her lips, and for a fleeting moment, she could almost feel Tasha's lips briefly brushing hers.

CHAPTER 15

WHAT IS LOVE

Tasha was not a Black Friday person. She was content to avoid the chaos and frenzy of shopping and simply enjoy a rare four-day weekend. Today was not cooperating. Megan seemed to be withdrawn, and Tasha couldn't seem to engage her. Eventually, Megan announced that she and Sophia were going to enjoy a bit of the cool, dry Friday at a nearby park, leaving Tasha to wonder what was wrong.

Everything seemed great yesterday. Megan seemed to have a good time at Friendsgiving. Sophia apparently enjoyed it as well. Did someone say something to her? Or was it something else? Was it that kiss? That was just an accident. It couldn't be that. More than anything, Tasha felt a hole in her heart that hadn't been there before.

After an hour in which Tasha felt increasingly adrift, Megan texted her. Megan was taking Sophia to Peet's Coffee for hot chocolate and wanted to know if Tasha wanted something. She texted back that she would like hot chocolate as well. With the way her nerves were going, coffee seemed like a bad idea.

Not long after that, Megan and Sophia returned with three hot chocolates. Megan got Sophia settled on the couch to watch *The Princess Switch*, where she was soon joined by Nocturne in a familiar cat and kid cuddle puddle. Meanwhile, Megan motioned Tasha over to the table and they sat down.

"I'm sorry, Tasha. It's been a weird morning for me."

"It's okay. Do you want to talk about it?"

"It's… I… Maria and I talked last night. I didn't know that she was a divorce lawyer."

"Did she advise you to…"

"Oh, no! Nothing like that. Actually, she said that I could talk with her if I wanted. We talked about other things, too. She said that I was good for you."

"What does that mean?"

"Um, it was a lot. Last night. She saw how much we loved each other. Not like that, I mean. As good friends and how you were so supportive and amazing."

As Megan's compliments rolled in, Tasha felt strangely depressed. "Of course I love you! We were roommates for four years. I was your maid of honor. We've been through a lot together and I've always got your back."

"I know, and I've always got yours, too. I'm just out of sorts because I know that I have to really think about what I'm going to do—what I feel, and what's best for Sophia."

Tasha nodded, waiting for her friend to go on.

"I'm so angry with Brad, but am I angry because I still love him or because I feel like a fool? He's Sophia's father, so I'm always bound to him by that, but I don't know that I can take him back. I don't know if I can divorce him, either. What will that do to Sophia? What about custody? Oh, god… what if he gets custody of Sophia? I don't…"

Tasha reached over and took Megan's hands in hers. She squeezed softly and said, "Just breathe. I'm here for you now, and I'll always be here for you. No matter what."

"You can't know that."

"Yes, I can. No. Matter. What. I will always be there. You are my ride-or-die."

"Thank you, Tasha. Thank you."

"Of course, sweetie. Anything for you. If you need to talk, then we'll talk. If you need a hug, then you'll get a hug. If you need to bury Brad's body somewhere in the mountains or deep under the Pacific where no one will ever find him, then I've got a butcher knife and a tarp."

"That last one is oddly specific."

"Definitely not something that I've spent the last six nights thinking about."

"Again, oddly specific." At least Megan was smiling again.

Tasha squeezed Megan's hands again. "I can't tell you what to do, but it might help to break your decisions into smaller chunks. Maybe start with how you feel about Brad?"

"Thanks, Tasha. That's usually how I go about things. I just got overwhelmed."

"I get that."

"Can I talk with you about love?"

"Of course."

"I mean, it's a hard question. What is love?"

"Oh, now you're gonna get that song stuck in my head."

Megan laughed. "Now I'll have it stuck in my head, too! But really, though, is it supposed to be a hard question? I feel like it's so easy in the movies or books."

"I dunno, I think it depends on the book."

"That's probably true. I mean, I love you. You're my best friend, but I let you slip away before, and does that mean that it wasn't real? I feel awful, you know. You were going through some really hard challenges in your life, and I wasn't there for you. But then, when my life goes to shit, you drop everything for me, and…"

"Oh, Megan. No, sweetie. We both messed up. I shoulda reached out to you after Momma stopped talking to me. I know that you would have supported me, because you're a good person and a good friend. It's my fault for not telling you."

"That makes me feel a little better. I'm really worried that maybe I'm not good at loving people."

"Sweetie, look at that little angel over there. You are plenty good at loving people, because I see just how much you love Sophia."

"Thank you, Tasha." Megan squeezed Tasha's hands back. "Okay, so maybe I'm not bad at loving. I'm still wondering, though. Do I love Brad? Did I ever really love Brad? He was handsome and charming. Still is, apparently. My mother thought that he was amazing. She was so excited when he proposed at our house during our last winter break. Did I say 'Yes' because I wanted to, or because everyone expected me to? Have the last ten years of my life been a waste because I just let things happen to me rather than taking control of my life?"

"Damn, that's a lot. One thing, though—those last ten years weren't a waste, you have Sophia."

"I know. She's the best thing that ever happened to me." Megan grinned. "Just slightly better than drawing you as my freshman year roommate."

"I'm even better than Lauren? Because that girl sends a good gift basket!" Tasha laughed as she watched her friend's face go beet red. She continued, "You're asking yourself some tough questions. What do you think?"

"I think… I think that I never loved Brad. And I don't think that he ever loved me. Not really. I think that we just did what was expected of us. What if I missed out on my soulmate because of this?"

"Ugh. There are seven billion people on the planet. No one has one perfect soulmate out of seven billion options. That doesn't mean that there isn't someone who is amazing for you out there. You just haven't met him yet." As Tasha finished that last sentence, two more words came unbidden from her brain, but died before they reached her lips. *Or her.*

CHAPTER 16
ORION

By the time she woke up on Saturday, Megan was feeling more confident about her future. Yesterday had been a difficult emotional roller coaster, but it had been helpful to dig into the complex issues that she was facing. She and Sophia slept on the air mattress again, although as she opened her eyes she noticed that she was now alone in the living room. Megan stood up and padded quietly to the bedroom door. Peeking in, she saw that Sophia had crawled into the bed and was sleeping peacefully next to Tasha. Her friend was awake as well, scrolling through her phone. Megan beckoned Tasha over while also signaling her to stay quiet.

The two adults reunited in the kitchenette a few minutes later. Megan noted that Tasha had moved from pajama pants and a long-sleeved nightshirt to pajama shorts and a tank top. She felt bad that Tasha had been uncomfortable about showing off her tattoos before.

"Good morning," Megan said quietly. She reached over to touch the cat pawprints on Tasha's left arm. "Where do these go?"

"Good morning to you." Tasha reached over to pull down the left strap of her tank top and lowered the shirt enough to show the cat paws coming to an end right above her heart. "You are now the third person to see where these end. Okay, fourth, including the woman who inked this. I adopted Nocturne right after I moved out here, and she has been such an important part of my life since then, I decided to get this done in her honor."

"Thank you for showing me. That's really sweet about Nocturne. She's a good cat."

"She is, but I think that she might like Sophia more."

"I'm sure that Nocturne still loves you, too. Did you sleep okay? I hope that Sophia didn't bother you."

"I slept fine. She didn't bother me at all. I didn't even hear her come in, so it was a surprise when I woke up and she was there."

Mgean gathered Tasha in for a hug. "Thank you for that. It means so much to me that you're okay with Sophia."

"Of course. Speaking of Sophia, there's a park nearby that might be nice for a walk and to give her a chance to play while the weather is still dry. Do you wanna go?"

"That's a great idea. Sophia should be up soon, and we can all go after breakfast."

Megan rummaged around in the refrigerator for a minute, then looked at Tasha who was watching her with a bemused smile.

Tasha asked, "Anything that you are looking for?"

"I'm thinking bacon and eggs with toast. Do you have any bread?"

"I like it. Would English muffins do?"

The smell of bacon brought Sophia out and the trio sat down for a nice hot breakfast.

Afterward, Megan and Sophia got ready together for their excursion with Tasha.

As they walked out of the apartment, none of them noticed the oversized pickup truck parked down the block. Nor did they see a man exit the truck and start to follow them.

It wasn't a long walk to the park. Once there, Megan and

Tasha sat on a bench and watched Sophia clamber up on the play-set. The two were idly chatting when Megan heard Sophia exclaim, "Mommy, look! Daddy's here!"

CHAPTER 17

SATURDAY NIGHT'S ALRIGHT FOR FIGHTING

Brad witnessed Megan immediately clutching Tasha's hand when she saw him standing next to the playground. *Oh, that's how it is,* he thought to himself. It was definitely time to remove Sophia from this sinful city and the wicked influence of Tasha. She had been a bad influence on Megan back in college, and Brad wasn't going to stand for this.

"Hello, Megan. Tasha."

Megan's face was ashen. "How did you find us?"

"You left your address book at our home and it wasn't hard to figure out where you would run." With palpable disdain, he added, "I see that this is where you have been keeping my daughter."

Tasha snapped, "What are you doing here, Brad?"

"Megan said that we would talk Saturday. Well, it's Saturday," Brad replied with a brash tone.

"No, Brad. Why are you stalking Megan at our home?"

Our home. Brad was unsurprised at Tasha's possessiveness. She had always been jealous of him. Well, he was here to bring his wife and child back home, and that was that. "It's not stalking. I drove all this way to reclaim what's mine. Anyway, I thought that this would be a good place to talk. Megan can't hang up on me in person." At this, Megan finally began to stir from stunned silence. "Besides, my daughter should be living in a safe and Christian home. Clearly, she is not."

Sophia was looking back and forth between her parents as Megan finally spoke, "Brad, this is not what I meant about talking today."

Finally, she speaks. Dad said that I just need to speak firmly to her and show her who is in charge. "Show her that you are the man," he told me.

Brad replied, "Well, this is what's best. You've had your little tantrum, now it's time to go home. Pack your things."

"No."

"No? I didn't give you that option!" Brad's mind went back to Thanksgiving day and his father's disappointment when he showed up without Megan and Sophia.

"What the hell, Bradley? Did I raise you to be a pussy?" his father had said.

Brad had stepped back in the face of his father's wrath. "I screwed up, Dad," he responded.

"How did you screw up?"

"Megan caught me with Margaret. We had a fight and she left."

Somehow, his father got angrier. "You bet your ass you screwed up! You let her leave instead of telling her what's what! You're supposed to be the man. You're a fucking idiot for getting caught, and you're a weakling for letting your wife walk all over you!"

Brad stood as tall as possible and assumed a power position to assert his male dominance.

"We're not going with you, Brad. Sophia and I are going to stay here with Tasha for a while and you can just leave."

Brad began feeling apprehensive. He was doing what his father said, but that wasn't working. It was time to try a new tactic. Appeal to her sense of duty and let her maternal instincts fill in the rest. "Really, Megan? You think that this city is a fit environment for a child? How big is your apartment? I'm guessing that it's small. Smaller now with three people crammed in it. Where are you even sleeping?"

"This is a great environment for Sophia. She's well taken care of, she likes playing with Tasha's cat. And we're managing the sleeping arrangements just fine."

"Oh, I bet you are." Brad glared suspiciously at Tasha.

"What are you implying?"

"Single woman with a cat in this god-forsaken city. You're probably happy to have another woman to share your sinful bed with."

"Screw you, Brad! Unlike you, Megan doesn't sleep around."

"And yet you don't deny wanting her in your bed!" Brad hadn't set foot in Portland since before the COVID hoax. After watching the city burn during the so-called Black Lives Matter protests, he knew that it wasn't a place for good people. He'd done a lot of research back then, not just on the fake vaccines, and learned a lot about this wicked city. The people that he communicated regularly with in the chatrooms told all sorts of stories about the horrors of Portland. No matter what it took, he was going to get his wife and child out of here and never return.

Brad knew that he was winning. Megan was withdrawn, letting Tasha speak in her stead.

One more appeal, this time to the ultimate truth, would win the day.

"Megan, you need to think about what's best for Sophia! She needs to be raised in a strong Christian home, with good Anglo-Saxon values."

Tasha snorted loudly. "Anglo-Saxon values? Brad, your last name is Kowalski. Your mother is half Italian. I am more Anglo-Saxon than you!"

"No, you're not! You're—"

"Black? Yeah, and my first ancestor on this continent arrived in South Carolina almost three hundred and fifty years ago... from England. Then he bought another of my ancestors off a boat from

Africa. And he raped her. Centuries of slavery, rape, and violence followed. That's my family history with Anglo-Saxon values!"

"But—"

"Brad, you best think carefully about the next words out of your mouth, because if you are about to spew some state of Florida revisionist bullshit about how slavery was good for Black folks, or how we liked picking cotton and singing fo' massa', then I will slap that nonsense right out of your mouth!"

Brad was flailing now. He was used to having conversations with people who agreed with him completely. Facing Tasha's righteous fury was unnerving. "Having one British ancestor doesn't mean you're Anglo-Saxon."

"Do you see my hair? No Black girl gets hair like this without a shitload of European genetics. Have you ever heard about one-drop laws? They were invented for families like mine. So you can take your Anglo-Saxon values and shove them up your ass, because I know *exactly* what that bullshit means."

Brad was stunned into silence. Megan whispered, "Brad, it's time for you to leave." As he gathered his wits, all three of them heard the sound of Sophia crying on the swingset. Brad was nearly knocked over as Megan bolted for her child. As he regained his balance, Tasha walked up to him and said in a deadly quiet voice, "You get the fuck out of here and don't you come back to our neighborhood. *Ever!*"

Minutes later, Brad sat shaking in the driver's seat of his truck. He'd screwed up badly. Really badly. He'd done what he thought he was supposed to do—what was right. So why didn't he win? *I'm so fucked.* Stanislaus Kowalski did not tolerate failure, and he certainly wouldn't tolerate weakness in his son. Brad's world had come crashing down around him, and he had no idea how to fix it.

CHAPTER 18
SYMPATHY FOR THE DEVIL

Tasha locked the door as soon as they got home, and then felt her legs go to jelly as the adrenaline faded. She couldn't remember the last time she had been that angry, but now that anger was quickly being forced back by concern. She looked into the bedroom to see Megan comforting Sophia on the bed, the two of them crying. Tasha felt her own heart break at the sight.

The next few hours were consumed by alternating waves of rage and misery. And lots of pacing. Nocturne emerged from under the couch and head-butted Tasha's legs briefly before going to the bedroom where her feline comforting skills were most needed.

Tasha fixed lunch for the three of them, delivering sandwiches to the bedroom, and then she collapsed wearily onto the couch. Today had been an emotional roller coaster, and Tasha felt exhausted.

Eventually, Megan emerged red-eyed from the bedroom, carrying two empty plates. She sat down next to Tasha on the couch. Tasha pulled Megan in, holding her the same way Megan had been holding her daughter not long before. Megan burrowed her head under Tasha's chin and stayed there. After a long time, she asked, "Is Maria as good as she says she is?"

"I mean, I haven't used her services myself, but I've met some of her former clients at various get-togethers. Yeah, I think she's probably as good as she says she is. Why?"

"I'm going to call Maria and get papers filed. I'm divorcing Brad."

"About fucking time… Sorry, that's not my place to say."

"It's okay. I probably should have dumped him the first time he cheated on me. I was just scared, though. I was pregnant. Taking him back, forgiving him… It was safe."

"I get that. Being a single mom sounds scary."

"Oh, I'm terrified right now!"

"Sorry, I didn't…"

"It's still new. I'll admit, I'm not as scared as I could be, because of you."

"You mean, free babysitting!"

"No, not that! Although… that sounds good, too."

They spent the next few minutes in a comfortable silence. Tasha sensed that Megan wasn't done talking, but she was done for the moment. She waited patiently for Megan to be ready, holding her friend close.

"Brad wasn't always like this, you know. I think I said before that he went to some bad places during COVID. Now I'm starting to feel that maybe he went further than I knew."

Tasha grunted in agreement. She'd tolerated Brad back in college only because he was dating Megan. After today, she was more than happy to never see him again.

Megan continued, "I need to help him, Tasha. Not for me, but for Sophia."

Tasha stiffened as she listened to Megan, who disentangled herself and sat up. Megan looked Tasha in the eyes and said, "I know that you hate him and I don't blame you. He was a complete asshole today, and I really hate him right now, too. That said, I believe it's important for Sophia to have a father that isn't a complete shitbag. And… I need your support. I know that this is a huge ask, and I don't need you to do anything. I just need to know that you have my back. Does that make sense? Am I crazy?"

"Ride or die, Megan. Ride or die. Yes, you make sense. No, you aren't crazy. Okay, a bit crazy, but in a good way. Look, I never liked Brad, and, yeah, I hate his guts right now..." Tasha paused, searching for the right words to say. "I'm not sure how to say this, so I hope that it comes out right. You are fucking amazing. After all of this. After today. After all the shit that Brad has put you through. You are willing to somehow try to help him pull his head from deep out of his ass, all for Sophia. And you're right. He was an over-privileged prick in college, but he wasn't the complete shithead that we saw today. I'm not sure how you deprogram a White boy who has been spending too much time in the fever swamps, but I will support you."

"Thank you, Tasha! Yeah, I have no idea how to deprogram him, either. I am going to try to figure out what to do. Of course, divorcing him at the same time isn't going to make it easier."

"Ain't that the truth! Come here." Tasha opened her arms again, and Megan returned to leaning into Tasha. They spent a long time like that, in thoughtful silence.

Megan was mildly shocked to realize that she had fallen asleep. She could feel Tasha's chin on her head and one of Tasha's arms still around her. Before she could say anything, she heard a small snore and realized that Tasha had fallen asleep, too. Megan smiled, and she had just closed her eyes again when she heard the unmistakable sounds of Sophia waking up and coming out of the bedroom. She tried to delicately extricate herself from Tasha, but her movement woke her friend.

"Hey."

"Hey."

"Thank you. I'm sorry that I fell asleep on you."

"That's okay. I think we all needed some rest after this morning."

"Yeah. I think you're right. I'm going to check on Sophia."

"Okay, I'm…," Nocturne hopped up into Tasha's lap, "...apparently not going anywhere."

Megan laughed as she walked toward the bedroom. "Hi, sweetheart. How are you feeling?"

"Better, Mommy."

"That's good. Come here and give your mom a hug." Megan

would have liked a longer hug with her daughter, but Sophia was quickly getting wiggly.

"You can talk to me about anything. You know that, right?"

"Yes, Mommy. I have to pee!"

Megan laughed. "Okay, go! I'll be out in the living room with Aunt Tasha." Out in the living room, Nocturne was making cat biscuits in Tasha's lap. As Megan sat down, Tasha grabbed the cat and placed her in Megan's lap.

"I gotta pee, too!" she exclaimed as she jumped up. Nocturne gave her human a baleful look before turning her head back to the important task of now making cat biscuits in Megan's lap.

"Oof, you're a pokey little lady." Megan said as she scratched Nocturne behind the ears. "Okay, time for you to get down. I have an idea." Nocturne gave a squeak as she was rudely interrupted and placed on the floor.

Megan quickly stripped the bed of sheets and pillows, then raided the closet for more. Tasha looked at her strangely as she lumbered into the living room with her arms overflowing. "Sophia, do you know what I think we need to do?"

"What?"

"I think that we need to make a pillow fort over here by the couch."

"Okay!"

The first effort collapsed unceremoniously; however, the second attempt fared better when Tasha suggested adding chairs to the construction. The final result wasn't so much a fort as something vaguely resembling a stall at a market, but that was perfectly fine. Tasha unplugged a stand lamp and placed it in the middle to make the sheet draped over the top convex rather than concave. In the epicenter of all of this, Nocturne supervised from her position exactly in the middle of the blanket on the floor.

Tasha microwaved popcorn and the trio watched movies. Megan offered to grab a bake-at-home pizza from Papa Murphy's. Tasha used that opportunity to get the oven started and feed Nocturne. Once Megan returned, they all settled in and watched a fun rom-com about a single dad who falls in love with a stranger, all orchestrated by his meddling daughter.

When Sophia started to fall asleep, Megan knew that this magic little moment was coming to an end. She and Tasha disassembled the pillow fort and remade the bed, with ample "assistance" from Nocturne. Then Megan left Tasha to play with Nocturne, who was having a grand time under the covers, so that she could get Sophia cleaned up and ready for bed. Once Sophia was tucked in, Megan went back to the living room and sat down next to Tasha.

"What a roller coaster of a day."

"Yeah, how are you feeling?"

"You know, pretty good, actually. As awful as Brad showing up unannounced was, deciding to divorce him has freed my mind. Yesterday, I felt buried under all of these questions. Don't get me wrong, I know that there are still a lot of questions and a lot of decisions ahead of me, but now I can at least see a path forward."

"I can understand that."

"I know that I've said this a lot, Tasha, but thank you so much. You have been amazing. You *are* amazing. I don't think that I could have done this without you."

"Yes, you could have. You're stronger than you give yourself credit for, Megan."

"Thank you for saying that. I mean, I could have done this alone, but I'm in a much better place right now because of you. We have a home because of you. This afternoon, the three of us together... You aren't just my best friend and Sophia's godmother. You're part of our family."

Tears welled up in Tasha's eyes as she reached over to hug Megan. As they hugged, Megan added, "You even let me fall asleep on you, which was amazing, by the way."

"Stop, you're going to make me cry!"

"Okay, I'll stop being mushy. Speaking of mushy, what's going on in this movie?" Another rom-com had started auto-playing and was about halfway done.

"Ummmm, I see a castle, so I'm betting there's a prince."

"Good call. I'm betting that she's American and the king... no, the queen disapproves."

"Probably wants him to marry some duchess or countess."

"Right... and she's a baker."

"Nope, that was *The Princess Switch*. Sophia watched that yesterday."

"She could still be a baker. Or maybe a chef."

"Should we restart it?"

"Nah, this is more fun!"

Once the movie ended, Megan looked over at Tasha and said, "I don't want you sleeping out here on the couch again."

"Really, it's fine."

"Come sleep in the bed with me and Sophia..."

"...and Nocturne..."

"I admit, it might be tight with the four of us, but after today, I don't know. It just feels... finding the right words is hard. Like, it would feel right to me if you were with us. You know, we should all be together... and stuff."

"That was very eloquent. Especially the 'and stuff' at the end. Really pulled the whole speech together." Tasha grinned.

Megan really did feel much better as she and Tasha climbed into bed, Sophia sleeping peacefully between them. Nocturne surveyed them with feline glee. She had always liked snuggling with her original human, and now she had two more to choose from. She decided to snuggle the smaller one first.

CHAPTER 20
COLD AS ICE

It had been a while since Tasha had shared a bed with anyone besides Nocturne. Her last few adventures in dating had generally not progressed to the point where a bed was involved. Neither of those that reached the bed stage ever progressed to the point where waking up the next morning happened. So it was very strange to feel someone pressed against her back when she woke up. It was definitely strange enough that the usual fog of sleep vanished instantly. As Tasha took stock of the situation, she realized that she could feel the familiar fuzzy warmth of Nocturne behind her knees. The form pressed against her back felt small. Sophia. And she could feel someone's feet touching hers. Megan. *Well, this is different. Good, though. Yes. Definitely good. Megan snores. I don't remember that from college. Then again, we never shared a bed in college. I think that's Megan snoring. Maybe it's Sophia. Nope, I feel her breathing against my neck. Definitely Megan, then.*

Tasha felt Megan's feet move away, and the gentle rhythm of Megan's snoring was broken as Tasha felt her shifting positions. More movement, and then Tasha felt a hand on *her* arm. The snoring resumed. *It's actually a kinda cute little snore. Not that I'm going to tell* her *that, of course. I feel like getting up would disturb everyone. And it's Sunday. I don't have to be anywhere. Besides, this is really nice.* Tasha closed her eyes again, drifting back to sleep with Megan's hand on her arm, Megan's snoring in her ears, and Sophia and Nocturne pressed against her.

A while later, Tasha woke up again to find herself alone in the bed. She walked into the living room a few minutes later.

"Good morning, sleepyhead! I was just telling Sophia how you were being lazy, sleeping so late."

"Was not!"

"Shhhhh!"

"Of course I slept late. I had to put up with your snoring half the night."

"I do *not* snore!"

"It was like sharing the bed with a bear."

"You lie!"

"It's true. Like a huge grizzly bear, snoring next to me. Isn't that true, Sophia?"

"Yeah! Huge!" Sophia shrieked with laughter.

"Now you're getting my own daughter involved in your lies."

"It's true, Mommy. You do snore. Maybe like a baby bear, though."

"Really? I snore?"

"Yeah. Sophia's right. Kinda like a baby bear. Cute, fuzzy little baby bear snores." Tasha grinned as Megan hid her blushing face in her hands. She reached out for Sophia's hand. "Let's go give your mom a hug. See, we're here to support you. Even though you snore."

"I'm so embarrassed."

"It's okay, Megan. You can't help that you snore. Just like you can't help having ice cold feet!"

"*What?*"

Tasha leapt back, cackling all the way, as she avoided getting swatted by Megan. "Okay, okay! Peace! I was just kidding about the ice cold feet. Mostly…"

"Ugh, and here I was going to fix you a nice, hot breakfast. I'm definitely not doing that for you now."

"What about me?" Sophia asked.

"Of course, angel. Your breakfast is coming right up. Do you think that I should make something for your mean Aunt Tasha?"

"Yes, Mommy. Aunt Tasha would like that."

"You're right, munchkin. Your Aunt Tasha would really like a nice, hot breakfast. And maybe your mom could make me some coffee, too."

"Now you're definitely pressing your luck."

"Fine… You win, grumpy girl. I'll make us coffee. Let me squeeze past you. Sophia, would you like your Aunt Tasha to make you some hot chocolate?" Tasha completely missed Sophia's answer as Megan pressed the sole of one foot against Tasha's calf. "Oh my god, your feet are ice cold!"

CHAPTER 21
YOU BELONG WITH ME

Megan really enjoyed having a relaxing and fun morning with her family. It was very strange to think of it that way. Just two weeks ago, her concept of family was so different. It wasn't that Tasha had replaced Brad, either. As much as she didn't like it, he was there and would always be there. Preferably just at a distance. A great distance would be nice. And Tasha... Tasha was an amazing friend and roommate. Their four years as college roommates were some of the best years of her life, and living with Tasha again just felt right. *That's what it is, right? Just great friends and great roommates? Definitely.* And yet... Megan struggled to figure out why that seemed wrong when it should be right. That was a conundrum for another day, though. Sophia was the one constant in her definition of family. And now she was about to risk everything.

"Sophia, I need to talk with you. This is important, okay?"

"Okay, Mommy."

Tasha heard the tone in Megan's voice, grabbed a book, and headed for the bedroom. "Sophia, I have decided that I am going to divorce your father. He broke a promise to me. A very important promise. And it is something that I can't forgive. Do you understand?"

"I think so. Does this mean that you won't live with Daddy anymore?"

"Yes. I won't live with Daddy anymore. When I came here, I wasn't sure what I was going to do, but I have decided now that I am going to live with Aunt Tasha. I'm not sure how long. I need to talk with her. But this is my new home. Does that make sense?"

"Yes, Mom. I like Aunt Tasha!"

"I do too. She is very special."

"Mom? Am I going to live with you?"

"That is something that I want to talk to you about. I am going to talk with your Dad about a lot of this, but you need to have a say in this, too. I want you to know that your father and I will always be in your life, but you may need to decide who you want to live with. That is a very hard decision to make, and it is a decision that I wish with all of my heart that you didn't have to make. I want you to know that I will love you no matter what, and I am sure that your dad feels the same way."

"That is very hard, Mommy."

"You don't have to decide now, okay?"

"Mom, what promise did Dad break?"

"Oh… um. When I married your dad, we promised each other that we would love each other and only each other. That's the promise that he broke."

"So, he loves someone else?"

"He says that he doesn't, but they were, um…"

"Was it sex stuff?"

"What? Where did you hear about that kind of thing?"

"Mom, I'm eight! Some of the kids at school talk about sex stuff."

"Okay, we are *definitely* going to have to talk about this soon. But not today. Yes, I caught your Dad doing… sex stuff… with another woman."

"Ew."

"Sophia. This is important. Just because your dad broke that promise to me, it doesn't mean that he doesn't love you. He loves you very much."

"When do I have to choose?"

"I don't know. Probably soon, but I don't know."

"If I live with Daddy, will I still see you?"

Megan's heart sank. "Of course, sweetheart. I will see you as much as I can. I don't know how often, but I promise you that I will see you every chance I get."

"Would Aunt Tasha come to see me, too?"

"I am sure that she would. I think that she loves you a lot."

They heard Tasha get out of bed and race to the bedroom door. "Of course I would come see you, Sophia!"

"What about Nocturne?"

"No, not Nocturne. I think that she really likes you, but cats don't usually like to travel."

"Maybe I should stay here, then. I like living with Aunt Tasha and Nocturne."

"You don't have to decide now, sweetheart. You know what helps me sometimes? I make two lists. On one list, I put down what I like most about one choice, and on the other I write down what I like most about the other choice. Then I compare the lists and see what is most important to me."

"That makes sense. I'll do that!"

"Take your time, okay? Maybe you can do that tomorrow after school."

"If I live with Daddy, will I have to go to school?"

"Yes, sweetie. You aren't getting out of school that easy."

"Okay." Sophia pouted, but Megan could see that her heart wasn't in it.

"Thank you for talking with me, Sophia. After dinner, would you like to go roller skating again?"

"Yes! That sounds fun. Mommy, can I play roller derby?"

"I might need to talk to your dad about that, but if you want to play, then I am okay with you playing."

"Do they have roller derby at our other home?"

"You mean where your dad lives? Let me look." Megan pulled out her phone and searched. "The closest roller derby league to your dad is in Bend, and that is still a long drive. It looks like they have a junior roller derby team, but it doesn't start until age ten."

"Oh, okay."

"What do you think, Sophia?" Megan said. "Should *I* try out for roller derby?"

"Mom! That would be so cool!"

"Who knows, maybe one day we could play roller derby together."

"That would be awesome! What about you, Aunt Tasha?"

"Your Aunt Tasha is happy to go roller skating with you, sweetie, but I messed up my knee playing soccer in college. I'm not sure that it would be safe for me to play roller derby. But I will *always* come watch you, okay?"

"Okay! I love you, Aunt Tasha!"

"I love you, too, Sophia."

CHAPTER 22
VENUS

Monday morning seemed to come far too soon. The teacher's strike had ended over the weekend and school was starting back up, with a two-hour delay on the first day back. All four of them woke up when Tasha's alarm went off. Megan looked across the red mop of Sophia's hair and said good morning to Tasha. "Did I keep you awake with my snoring?" she asked with mock petulance.

"Good morning, and no. You only snored like a small bear last night, so I slept just fine."

Megan grunted at that, then poked her daughter. "Come on, sleepyhead. Let's get ourselves going. Just remember that we need to let Aunt Tasha get ready because she has to leave first, okay?"

There were a series of unintelligible mumbles from under the blankets, but Sophia did start to move. What followed was a whirlwind of activity as three humans and one cat got ready for the day. Nocturne was by far the easiest, as she just needed her breakfast and then an energetic round of post-poop-zoomies before she was ready for a long day of napping. The three humans engaged in a delicate dance to share one bathroom, get breakfast, get dressed, and then get out the door.

Megan walked Sophia to school, where she saw the principal greeting students as they returned to school for the first time since Halloween. They had a brief conversation, and the principal promised to keep an eye out for Sophia that day to make sure that she settled in okay. Feeling better, Megan headed downtown to the Portland Public Schools main offices. She arrived to find an ugly orangish-pink building whose architectural style could best be described as a bureaucratic blockhouse.

She got her paperwork squared away with HR and her photo taken at security. As a teacher transferring within the state, she was already background-checked and had all of her qualifications, so the whole process was mostly painless. After waiting a bit for her new ID badge, Megan was ready to go. Tasha had been right about PPS' desperate need for substitutes—she already had an assignment booked at McDaniel High School the next day.

During the wait for her ID badge, Megan dug Maria's card out of her purse and called her number. Maria greeted her warmly, and she kindly offered to buy Megan lunch. "Don't even worry about it, I can write it off as a business expense," Maria said. They met for lunch at Dar Salam, an Iraqi restaurant. Megan took Maria's suggestion to start with the adis soup, which turned out to be excellent.

Over the course of their meal, Megan and Maria discussed her divorce and what Megan's goals were. Maria made sure to emphasize that giving Sophia a choice could end with Sophia choosing Brad. Throughout the meal, Maria kept up a steady stream of questions, probing Megan's goals and concerns, all the while taking copious notes. At the end, she tore off a sheet of paper and handed it to Megan, saying, "These are the outstanding questions that I need you to answer. I know it seems like a lot, but it isn't really. I know your primary goals and requests. It's unusual, but not unheard of. I hope that all of this can be settled amicably, but that decision lies with your soon-to-be ex-husband."

"Thank you, Maria. And, thank you for lunch."

"You are quite welcome. I really enjoyed meeting Sophia at the party. I'm having a similar event for Christmas, and you both are invited. All three of you, actually. Please pass along my invitation to Tasha. I trust that the two of you are still getting along well."

"Very well, and thank you for the invitation. That sounds wonderful!"

"Again, you are very welcome. The Christmas party should be a grand time." Maria checked her watch. "I do have to run, though. I have a meeting with another client soon."

"Thank you again. Have a great day, Maria!"

After their lunch, Megan headed back home, where Nocturne greeted her by falling down on her side and rolling around. She spent a good amount of time scratching the cat, who was seemingly starved for attention. Eventually, Megan fell for the classic tummy trap. Nocturne showed Megan her belly, and it looked so fuzzy and inviting, but when Megan went to rub that fuzzy tummy, Nocturne was greatly displeased. Megan was left inspecting her hand for signs of blood as Nocturne stalked off to the couch in a huff. Megan decided that Nocturne must have given her the warning claws rather than the full blades of death.

There was one last thing to do today before she walked over to school to meet Sophia. Megan picked up her phone and opened her contacts. *Don't pick up, don't pick up, don't pick up... Yes! Voice-mail!* After the beep, Megan said, "Hey, Brad. We need to meet and talk. Maybe this weekend. Don't pull a stunt like Saturday again. I will email you and we can discuss a time and place."

She made it to Sophia's school a few minutes early, and hung out awkwardly near some other parents. They all seemed to know each other, and Megan felt like she was an outsider.

She breathed a sigh of relief when she heard the bell. She resolved to go to a PTA meeting or something soon so that she could introduce herself. She watched the wave of students exit the building, searching for Sophia. Sophia came out with the principal and both walked over to Megan. "Hi, sweetheart, did you have a good day?"

"Yes, Mom. Everyone seemed nice."

"I kept an eye out for Sophia and checked in with her teachers. She seems to be settling in well so far," the principal said.

"Thank you, you really didn't have to do that!"

"Starting at a new school mid-year is stressful. I try to look out for those students whenever possible. We all do. The teachers here are amazing."

"Speaking of, I'm a sub now, so if you ever need someone to cover…"

"Thank you. I will keep that in mind. Are you looking for permanent work or just subbing?"

"I'm thinking about something permanent, but I have a lot going on right now, so…"

"Understandable."

Megan felt a tug on her arm. "Okay, it seems like we need to go. Thank you again for keeping an eye out for Sophia."

"You're welcome."

"Okay, let's get you home, munchkin. What did you have for lunch?"

"PBJ!"

"Yum, what other things did they have?"

Megan let Sophia talk about her day, enjoying her excitement about the new school, asking questions as needed. The walk home was very pleasant. Rain was coming soon, but today was a good day.

Back home, Megan got Sophia settled in. They spent some time together before Megan started on dinner. Tasha had texted to say that she would be late, so Megan decided to make a turkey pot pie. She enlisted Sophia's help, teaching her how to make a pie crust and roll it out. Then they cut some vegetables and diced the last of the turkey from the Friendsgiving leftovers.

Dinner was ready right before Tasha walked through the door. "Honey, I'm home!" Tasha said with a tired smile.

"Welcome home. Dinner's ready."

"It smells amazing."

"Wine?"

"Yes… You are the best!"

"Goddess?"

"Hey now, there's only one of those in this household and that's me." Tasha smiled and added, "Demi-goddess?"

"Hmm, I think maybe the goddess title should go to whoever does the most recent nice thing."

"Maybe… Fine, I guess that you can have the title for now."

Nocturne meowed.

"And yes, you are always a little goddess, aren't you?"

After dinner, Megan got Sophia ready for bed and tucked her in. She found Tasha on the couch, trying to find something to watch. "Thank you for dinner. It tasted amazing, especially after the day that I had."

"Rough one?"

"It wasn't hard. Just two big clients emailing me about changes all day long, plus stupid Kevin is back, so he had to chime in. Ugh."

"I'm sorry, Tasha. Shoulders or feet?"

"Huh?"

"Probably shoulders. Turn around."

"Wuh?"

Megan sat behind Tasha and dug her hands into Tasha's shoulders, working out the knots of tension she found.

"Goddess… definitely goddess…"

CHAPTER 23
WE FOUND LOVE

Tuesday was a regular school day, so everyone woke up when Megan and Tasha's alarms went off simultaneously. Tasha fell back to her pillow thinking, *Good news, two alarms means that I'll get to work on time for sure. Bad news, I can't push the snooze button on an alarm that requires reaching across two people and a cat.*

She lay there with her eyes closed, listening to Megan as she tried to rouse Sophia. *If someone had told me two weeks ago that I would be sharing my bed with another woman and an eight-year-old, I would have told them that they were crazy. It's not bad, though. Actually, it's really nice. I'm really glad that I bought a queen-sized bed, though. Seemed frivolous at the time, but it's paying off now. It's definitely very cozy. I should think about a king-sized bed. Uh oh, Sophia is finally getting up. I better pee before Megan hogs the bathroom.*

With a newly found urgency, Tasha got up and started her day. The whirlwind of activity was a bit more familiar today. She made coffee while Megan coached Sophia through the process of feeding Nocturne, a task made more difficult by Nocturne's insistence on sticking her head into every step of the process. Tasha was getting familiar with Sophia's morning routine, so she jumped in when she could, getting a relieved smile from Megan in return. While Sophia was brushing her teeth, Tasha poked her head into the bedroom. "Why don't I walk Sophia to school today?"

"Really, won't you be late?"

"Nah, there's a bus stop near the school. I can drop her off, hop the bus, and still get to work on time."

"Are you sure?"

"Absolutely. It would be my pleasure."

"Thank you, Tasha. That would be a huge relief. Oh, hey, sweetie. You're going to get breakfast at school today, alright?"

The productive chaos continued until Megan had to leave. "Okay, Sophia. Mommy has to go to work now. Do you have everything? Your bag is packed. Do you have the keys? Are you sure that you know how to walk home?"

"Mom!" Sophia huffed. "I'm a big girl and it's only four blocks. I can do it."

"I just worry about you. You're my angel. Your Aunt Tasha is going to walk you to school, okay?"

"Okay!"

"Alright, I gotta go! Tasha, thank you! Sophia, I love you!" With that, Megan was heading out the door.

Tasha watched her go, then turned to finish getting herself ready. She helped Sophia into her coat and got her arms into the straps of her backpack. "Got your keys, munchkin?"

"In my backpack, Aunt Tasha."

"Okay, don't lose them."

"I won't!"

With that, she grabbed her coat and they headed for the door. Tasha locked the door behind them. As she put her keys in her coat pocket, she felt a small hand grab her free hand. Tasha looked down. Sophia was looking up at her with an impish grin on her face.

"I love you, Aunt Tasha."

Those five words, uttered with the guileless sincerity of a child, changed Tasha's whole life. In that instant, she knew that she would do anything to keep this family together.

Nine years before that, when Megan had asked Tasha to be the godmother to her future child, Tasha hadn't really given much thought to what that really meant. Now she knew. Tasha had never really felt the need to have children, but this child holding her hand and looking at her with love, expectation, and a hint of devilish delight dancing in her eyes was a part of her now, and she would never let go.

"I love you, too, angel."

"Mommy calls me angel."

"I know. Is it okay if I call you angel?"

"Yes, Aunt Tasha."

"Good, I like that."

They walked hand-in-hand to Sophia's school. As she was about to leave, someone who matched Megan's description of the principal came out and greeted her.

"Hi, are you Sophia's other mother?"

"I, um… No, Megan and Sophia are living with me. I'm Tasha."

"Good to meet you, Tasha. It's very nice of you to walk Sophia to school."

"I'm happy to do it. Megan is subbing over at McDaniel today, so since she had to leave early, I walked Sophia to school. I gotta run to catch my bus. Good meeting you."

"You too."

Tasha often spent her bus rides to work mentally preparing for the day ahead. Today, though, she was deep in thought about this morning and how she just felt… different. She hadn't had family in her life for years now. She hadn't spoken with her parents since before she left South Carolina. She heard from her brother, Dante, every once in a while, mostly when she wanted to know how her parents were doing. Dante had his own family, though, back on the East Coast.

Megan had talked about the three of them as a family. On Friendsgiving, Maria had talked with her about "found family" and how important that could be. Today, for the first time, Tasha really felt what that meant. Sophia was part of her family now, not by blood, but by heart and soul. Megan, too. She smiled as she reflected on how she and Megan had traded off this morning, each helping Sophia get ready while the other focused on her own needs. They really were a good team. Megan was an amazing mother, and now Tasha felt a sliver of what being a mother was about. She liked the idea of being Sophia's unofficial other mother.

Once at work, Tasha's day was a shitshow. She was fielding emails from clients and prioritizing how to get their needs fulfilled when Kevin dumped another project on her. She had been cruising along, listening to Sade, but now she needed to pump things up to eleven if she was going to get this done. It was Motörhead time. A few hours later, she was starting to see the light at the end of the tunnel. Tasha ate a quick lunch and texted Megan, telling her that she would be making them spaghetti that night and asking if Megan could handle the garlic bread for her. After that, the headphones went back on, with N.W.A. on the playlist. Tasha ended the day with Aretha, and somehow she managed to get everything done on time.

On her way home, Tasha was finally able to check on personal things. Megan was taking care of the garlic bread and reported that Sophia made it home from school without incident.

There was an email from Lauren. Her check was on the way, and Lauren had found her some new business. Apparently, there were quite a few woman-owned adult boutiques around the country, and some of those businesses were interested in having Tasha make some website upgrades. Lauren also asked how she and Megan liked the "gift basket" that she had sent them. Tasha responded to thank Lauren and say that Megan had really enjoyed the gift basket but that she had not had the opportunity to try anything out yet. She added that there were some items that she was unfamiliar with and wasn't sure how to use. Her phone dinged as she exited the bus—Lauren had emailed some videos. *Oh, I'm gonna need some privacy for this.*

Once Tasha was home, she greeted everyone before getting started on dinner. "Hey, Megan, how was your first day?"

"It was good. Really good. The front office staff were super nice when I got to the school. The principal was greeting students as they entered and he was very friendly. He gave me directions to my classroom. Oh my god, that school… it's more like a college building."

"Really?"

"Yeah, it was rebuilt a couple of years ago. Sophia's school is old and kinda looks like it, but this high school was still shiny. The kids were generally good, too. You hear horror stories about high school, but I liked it. I'm over at Irvington tomorrow. It's an elementary school."

"That's great. I'm really happy that you had a good day."

"Me too. Oh, so we made garlic bread like you asked. I also showed Sophia how to make meatballs. I put them in the fridge."

"Nice, thank you. You're really getting into showing Sophia how to cook."

"Yeah. Brad's a meat and potatoes guy, so I never felt inspired before. Now, though, I'm having fun and it's great to share that fun with Sophia."

"That's awesome. Speaking of awesome, do you know what she did this morning?"

"What?"

"As we were leaving for school, she took my hand and told me that she loved me."

"Aw, that's adorable."

"Hey, Megan." Tasha looked her best friend in the eye and took a deep breath. "You know how you were talking about us as a family?"

"Yeah…"

"I really feel that, too. And… I… I guess today it hit me… I feel like Sophia is a little bit like my daughter, too. Does that sound weird?"

"Oh, Tasha!" Megan exclaimed as she crushed Tasha in a bear hug. "That's not weird. It's beautiful. I want us to be a family."

"I'd like that, too. I also need to breathe."

"Oh, sorry! How was your day?"

"Long. I got through it, though. Oh, I got an email from Lauren. Some other shops like hers need website upgrades and now I've got some extra business."

"Nice! Women helping women. I like it!"

"Oh, she asked how we liked her 'gift basket.' I told her that you enjoyed it a lot."

"Tasha." Megan blushed. "Hmmm, tomorrow night is an open skate night at the roller rink. Maybe I'll take Sophia roller skating and you can try out what Lauren sent." Megan gave her a devilish grin.

"I can't believe you said that! Actually, I can. You know what, I am going to take you up on that offer. I haven't had any stress release lately."

"Oh, is that what we're calling it now? Stress release?"

"Yes, stress release. Do I need to buy new batteries?"

"Not everything needs… Hey! I'll show you how I like to release stress."

Tasha had to dance, duck, and dodge to avoid Megan's attempts to tickle her in revenge, laughing all the while.

CHAPTER 24

I WANT TO KNOW WHAT LOVE IS

Getting ready on Wednesday morning was a little less chaotic than the day before. They were learning how to be around each other, starting to build a routine. Megan was immensely grateful to have Tasha jumping in to help Sophia get ready. It wasn't a seamless process, but it was getting better. Megan was able to find a moment when neither of them needed to supervise to talk with Tasha.

"Hey, so, tonight Sophia and I are going roller skating."

"Um, yeah. Thank you… Speaking of, I'm at the cat shelter this Saturday. Why don't I take her with me and you can stay here for some stress release?"

"I guess that stress release is a thing now… That's fine. Um… There's something else that I want to ask you, and you can say 'no.'"

"Uh huh…"

"I'm still struggling with the whole 'Do I really love Brad?' thing and I wanted an outside opinion on defining love." Megan paused, then continued in a rush, "So, is it okay if I call your mom?"

"Wait, what? Why Momma? Why not your parents?"

"My parents hate each other, but they're both stubborn

Catholics who refuse to get divorced, so they live in misery. Your parents, though—I know they have their moments, but they always seemed to have a genuine love for each other."

"Yeah, even at your wedding, your parents barely seemed to tolerate each other. Um, let me think about it, okay?"

"Okay, let me know."

With that, their interlude ended and it was back into the fray, getting themselves and Sophia ready. Megan left earlier than the day before, deciding to take the bus over to Irvington Elementary. The day went fairly well, and during an afternoon prep period, she saw that she had a message from Tasha.

> Tasha: I'm sending you Momma's home and cell number. I double checked with Dante to make sure that they were right. Good luck.

> Megan: Thank you!!! :)

Once she was home, Megan helped Sophia with her schoolwork and chatted with her about her day. Nocturne curled up in her lap, which was very comforting, but also meant that she couldn't move. Eventually, though, Nocturne got up and sought out Sophia's lap, allowing Megan to grab her phone and call Tasha's mom.

"Hello?"

"Hi, Mrs. Washington. I don't know if you remember me—it's Megan Kowalski."

"Megan! Of course I remember you! And call me Estelle."

"Thank you, Estelle. Um, you're probably wondering why I'm calling…"

"Is it Tasha? Is she okay?"

"Oh, yeah… No. Tasha is good. She's doing well."

"So, you've seen her?"

"Yeah, actually, my daughter and I are living with her right now."

"Are you alright?"

"Yes… No… Kinda both. Brad cheated on me and I left him. Tasha is letting us stay with her for a little bit."

"Hmm. Tasha never liked that boy… I'm sorry to hear about that."

"Thanks. It's been a rough couple of weeks, but Tasha is a great friend, which makes things better."

"Uh huh. Are you going to try to work things out with Brad, or are you done?"

"Definitely done."

"Well, I don't know any lawyers in Oregon, but I know half the lawyers in South Carolina and I'm sure that one of them knows a good divorce lawyer in Oregon."

"Oh, thank you, Estelle. That's very kind, but I have a divorce lawyer already. She's a friend of Tasha's."

"How did Tasha meet a divorce lawyer?"

"Um…"

"Never mind. I'm glad that she's doing well. Now you were about to tell me why you called."

Relieved that she didn't have to figure out how to explain how Tasha knew Maria, Megan said, "I've been struggling lately to understand love. My parents have always been terrible role models, but you and Mr. Washin… Um, John. You and John seem to have a genuine love for each other. What makes it work for the two of you?"

"Well, it's not always sunshine and roses, you know."

"I know."

"We get along because we are honest with each other. We trust each other. We are always there for each other. It's more than that, though. We have a deep emotional bond."

"I always saw that between you two. How did you know? Like, before you got married."

"Oh, honey. That was a long time ago. We met in college. I was pre-law and he was an English major. We met at a Black student union mixer. He was very shy, but handsome." Estelle laughed. "I caught him looking at me all night and I finally went up and talked to him because he clearly wasn't making the first move."

"Wow, that's awesome."

"You know that I am a tigress!" Estelle laughed again, then continued. "We ended up talking the rest of the evening. He was very charming—once he opened his mouth, of course. I gave him my number and told him that he better call me. He did. John! John, come over here. It's Megan. Tasha's friend from college. She wants to know how we fell in love."

Megan heard rustling on the other end of the line, then a man's voice. "Hello?"

"Hello, Mr. Wa— John."

"How are you, Megan?"

"I've been better, but I know that things could be worse and I'm grateful for what I have. How are you?"

"I'm grand! How's that little girl of yours? I always loved her name. Sophia, the Greek word meaning wise, clever, smart. I would have named Tasha that, but Estelle got to name the girls."

"Well, I guess that explains Dante's name then."

"One of my favorites. Now, Estelle said that you wanted to know how we fell in love. Is that right?"

"Yes, sir."

"Pffft, you don't have to 'sir' me." John laughed heartily. "I remember this like it was yesterday. When we were in college, I went to one of the mixers and there across the room, was the most beautiful woman I had ever seen. I felt like Eros had shot his arrow straight into my heart."

"Eros?"

"The Romans called him Cupid and made him a baby with tiny wings. I prefer the Greek version. Anyway, I was shocked when she came up to me. We talked all night long. She was as intelligent as she was beautiful. Estelle gave me her number. I called her the next day, but I suspect that she might have tracked me down if I hadn't. We started dating, and by the end of that first date, I knew that I couldn't live without her."

From the background, Megan heard, "You better believe it!"

John continued, "As beautiful as she was on the outside, I discovered that she was more beautiful on the inside. Her intelligence, compassion, humor… I couldn't help but be forever in love with her."

"That's amazing, thank you."

"Here, I'm gonna give you back to Estelle. Dante's family is coming over for dinner and I need to get the grill started."

"Okay, thank you, John. Hi again, Estelle."

"Well, now you have John's side of the story. He called me the next day to ask me out. We met at a restaurant just off campus. Megan, he was so nervous! It was cute, but I was a bit worried at first. Then, once we got to talking, I saw how smart and confident he could be. It's funny, he's always been so confident as a teacher and a church leader, but even today, he's still kinda shy around me. Like he can't believe how lucky he is."

Megan laughed. "He really is lucky. You're an amazing woman, Estelle!"

"Well, thank you, sugar. So, we dated for a while, but we both knew early on that this was forever. Our lives haven't always been easy, and there have been challenges, but everything has always been easier because we were there for each other."

"Thank you, Estelle."

"You're welcome, honey. Did this help?"

"It did. It helped a lot. I've really been struggling with my feelings toward Brad. I wanted to know if what we had was really love or not. Does that make sense?"

"It does. It's difficult to ask questions like this of ourselves, and I respect that you are doing that. I also respect that you are wise enough to seek help, too. Too many people are too proud to ask for help. I know, because I can be one of them. I haven't spoken to my own daughter in years. I miss her, Megan, but I…"

"I think that she misses you, too."

"You didn't call to talk about my problems. What have you decided about Brad?"

"Oh, um… I think I loved the idea of being married, and Brad checked off the right boxes at the time, but I don't believe that we had true love. Certainly not like you and John. Thank you so much, Estelle."

"You're very welcome, Megan."

"Hey, I should let you go since I know that Dante is coming over soon. Say 'hi' to him for me, okay?"

"I will. Thank you for your call."

"Honey… I'm home."

"Is that…"

"Yes." Megan impulsively stood up and bolted for the door. She mouthed, "your mom" at Tasha before she shoved her phone into Tasha's hand.

"Hello?"

Megan could faintly hear Estelle's voice answer.

"Momma… I missed you, too."

Megan quietly backed away, leaving the two of them to reconnect, hoping that she had done the right thing.

CHAPTER 25

THAT'S WHAT FRIENDS ARE FOR

About an hour later, Megan and Sophia headed out for roller skating. Tasha wearily handed over Megan's phone and said, "You two have fun." She added, "Megan, can we talk later? It's okay, I just need to talk."

"Yeah, Tasha. Of course. Alright, let's go, sweetheart."

"Bye, Aunt Tasha!"

"Bye, munchkin."

Megan did her best to have a good time roller skating with Sophia. She wouldn't normally keep her out this late on a school night, but she figured that Tasha might need some space right now. She was also worried that she might have done the wrong thing by putting Tasha and Estelle on the phone together. At least part of the reason for keeping Sophia out late was her anxiety about Tasha's reaction.

When they finally got home, Sophia was already half-asleep, which made getting into bed easier in some ways and harder in others. Once that was accomplished, she nervously went out and sat with Tasha.

"Hey."

"Hey."

"How are you doing?"

"I'm fine, I think."

"Uh oh. Any time I told Brad I was fine, I was never fine."

"No, it's good. Really. I'll admit that I was taken aback when you shoved your phone in my hand. But… thank you for doing that. Momma and I have both been so stubborn about this. I don't know if we would have talked any other way."

"I'm sorry, Tasha. I shouldn't have forced that on you. You told me how you haven't talked with your parents in years and I should have respected that, but I was talking with your mom and she sounded like she really missed you but couldn't see her own way to reaching out to you, so I just—"

Tasha held up her hand to stop her. "Megan, really, it's good. Momma and I had a good talk. I missed her so much, but was too stubborn to pick up the phone… Megan, I told her about dating… about dating women. About *me* dating women."

Megan grabbed Tasha's hands and squeezed.

"She didn't say anything for a minute when I told her. I thought I had ruined everything again. And then Momma told me it was okay. She told me that she didn't care about any of that, just so long as I found happiness and love."

"That's amazing, Tasha. That was very brave of you!"

"Thank you. I almost chickened out."

"You didn't, though. You were honest, and I know that your mom respects that."

"I feel like such an idiot. We missed so much time because of stupid pride. I talked to Dad for a bit, too. It was so nice to reconnect with both of them."

"That's so good to hear, Tasha."

"And now I'm in this weird place where I'm happy and sad at the same time. But, how was your talk with Momma?"

"It was really helpful for me. Your parents are so cute! It's different, but I also feel like I've wasted so much time."

"I'm glad that they could help you."

"Me too. I really hope that one day I find love like they have."

"Yeah, I'd like that, too. Megan, can I ask you for a favor?"

"Of course, Tasha. Anything?"

"I miss having Momma hold me. Can you hold me like I did for you a few days ago? I just need that right now."

"Of course! Come here and Mama Megan will make it all better."

"Okay, don't make it weird."

"Sorry."

Once she finished snuggling next to Megan, Tasha asked, "So, what's going on with Brad?"

"That… Well, after my meeting with Maria, she had some questions that I needed to answer. I sent her those answers earlier today. So, now she's working on drawing up the documents. I'm planning to meet Brad on Sunday after lunch. I'm really worried, though."

"Why?"

"Because he's promised so many things to me and then broken my trust. I'm worried that he'll tell me that he'll make these changes to be a good father to Sophia and that I'll believe him, only to be betrayed again."

"Yeah, I get that."

They stayed like that for a while, just enjoying each other's presence and the companionable silence.

Eventually, Tasha stirred and said, "Megan, I have a thought."

"Hmmm?"

"Let me meet Brad on Sunday."

"What? Why?"

"You said it yourself. You trust him too easily. Me, on the other hand, I never liked that boy and I never trusted him. I love… I love Sophia with all my heart and I will never let Brad hurt her, or you, if I can help it. So, let me help. Brad can't bullshit me. That rudeness and arrogance that he showed in the park isn't going to fly. And we both know where he was going with that 'Anglo-Saxon values' trash, too. That boy is a toxic mix of racism and sexism right now, and neither of you need that in your life. So, if I believe him that he's gonna get his shit together for Sophia's sake, then you'll know it's true."

"You'd do that for Sophia?"

"Damn right I would! I would walk through Hell for that girl. You best believe that I consider talking with Brad to be at least a bit of Hell."

"Thank you, Tasha. Let me think about that."

"Sounds good. Oh, while I talk to Brad, you can take Sophia to roller derby. There's a juniors doubleheader on Sunday."

"That's a good idea. Either way, one of us should take her to that."

"Okay, we need to go to bed. If I stay here any longer we are never gonna leave."

"This is nice, though, right?"

"It is. Anyone ever told you that your boobs make good pillows?"

"*What?*"

Tasha grinned devilishly at Megan as she untangled herself from her. "Just sayin'. Definitely more comfortable than my regular pillow."

"Stop, or I'll never give you Mama hugs again," Megan whined at her.

"Yes, Mom," Tasha replied, perfectly imitating Sophia's 'exasperated by mom' tone. Tasha giggled as she ducked a flying throw pillow.

CHAPTER 26

ALL I WANT FOR CHRISTMAS IS YOU

Thursday passed relatively uneventfully as everyone settled into their new routine.

Friday morning, Tasha got a minute alone with Megan. "Hey, today's the first day of December, and, uh, is Sophia going to be worried about…" her voice dropped to a whisper, "Santa finding y'all?"

"Oh, good thought, but we're in the clear on that. She figured out the whole Santa thing last year."

"Okay, good. What about a tree? Should we get one?"

"I thought you said that you were an atheist."

"So? I still like Christmas."

"Let's talk later, alright?"

"Oh, can you get groceries today? I can send you a list later. I want to teach Sophia how to make samosas."

"Oh, I'd like to learn that too. Send me the list."

With that, they were off to face the day. Megan was soon out the door. Tasha and Sophia left a little later to walk to school. Once she got to work, Tasha put on her headphones and let LL Cool J help make work go faster.

During lunchtime, Tasha sent Megan a shopping list. Near the end of lunch, she received the all-staff invite to the company holiday party next Friday, followed almost immediately by an over-enthusiastic missive from Kevin telling everyone how showing up was a sign of being a "team player." Looking at the invite, Tasha hatched a plan for a fun girl's night. Once she decided, she called Maria.

"Maria, hi!"

"Tasha, dear! How are you?"

"I'm good. This is a bit weird, but maybe you know someone who knows someone. Um, I need a babysitter."

"Really? You weren't even showing last week."

"Ha. Ha. You're hilarious. Actually, it's for Sophia. My company's holiday party is next Friday, and I want to bring Megan."

"Oh, like a date?"

"No, no. We're friends. Um, I haven't even asked her yet, actually."

"When does your party start, and where is it?"

"It starts at six, and it's at a local lounge near work. Why?"

"Hmm. Sophia is a darling girl. I have a proposition for you, my dear."

"What?"

"I will babysit Sophia next Friday night if Megan can bring her over immediately after school."

"That would work. I'll ask Megan, but I'm sure she'll agree."

"Excellent. I have one other condition."

"Uh, sure. What is it?"

"You must wear that red minidress that you wore at Friendsgiving."

"What? Really? Why?"

"Because you looked stunning in that dress, that's why."

"I did look good. Fine, I can do that."

"Lovely! I'll have a grand time with Sophia and you must send me selfies from your party."

"I will! Thank you, Maria!"

"You're very welcome, Tasha. Have a wonderful day!"

"You, too! Bye!"

Once her lunch was over, Tasha tuned into some Diana Ross. At three, Kevin scheduled a team meeting to, as he said, "Get everyone pumped up to finish this year strong." The meeting was as depressing and demotivating as Tasha imagined it would be, yet somehow Kevin seemed to think it was an immense success. She sometimes wondered how anyone could be that detached from reality.

After the meeting was finally over, she let Gloria Gaynor remind her that she would survive. After the message of hope, she got into some early Madonna, followed by Blondie. Then, as the clock ticked interminably toward five thirty, she put on Loverboy's "Working For the Weekend" to help her endure those last few minutes.

She got lucky with the bus, having a minimal wait time and a short commute. Once home, she gave Sophia a big hug, gave Nocturne some uncomfortable (for a cat's dignity) cuddles, and then gave Megan a quick hug too.

"Ugh, I am so glad it's Friday!"

"Me too!"

"How was your day?"

"Really good. The kids were relatively well behaved. I got a new assignment—I'll be over at Grant next week. How was your day?"

"Eh, it was okay. Kevin gave us a motivational speech," she said with a shudder.

"Oh, I bet you feel truly motivated now!" The sarcasm in Megan's tone ran very deep.

"Let me guess, You've been motivated like this before?"

"Yes, I have. Please tell me that there was a presentation, with lots of pictures and motivational quotes!"

"Ugh, thankfully no. Please don't give Kevin any ideas. Speaking of… my company's holiday party is next Friday night. Would you be my plus one?"

"I'd love to, but I'd have to—"

"Already ahead of you. Maria said that she would watch Sophia."

"Really? Divorce lawyer and babysitter? That's interesting."

"Yeah, about that. She said that she needs you to bring Sophia over right after you both get out of school."

"Huh, that's weird. That's fine, I guess. Did she say why?"

"No, but Maria can be—" Tasha paused, searching for the right words. "Not crazy. When you're rich, it's eccentric."

"Oh, shit, I never asked her what her fees were."

"Seriously?"

"I was focused on other things. I don't think she brought it up." Megan was looking panicked.

Tasha said soothingly, "Well, hopefully she gives you the 'friends and family' discount. It's not like she needs the money. She did a few divorces for the ex-wives of tech billionaires, so I'm pretty sure that she's already set for life."

"I'll ask about fees when I see her next. She had the papers delivered today."

"Oh, good. You and Sophia don't have issues with shrimp, right?"

"Yeah, I would have said something once I saw it on your list."

"Cool. I'm gonna make us shrimp scampi for dinner tonight."

"That sounds great, can I do anything?"

"Nah, it's simple. Just hang out and chat, unless you need to tend to Sophia."

Megan turned her head to observe her daughter. "Nope, she looks happy. She's reading and Nocturne looks to be settling in for a nap."

"Good. It's nice to talk with you. Feels domestic. In a good way."

"Yeah. Oh, about Christmas. Do you celebrate?"

"Sort of. I may not believe anymore, but the important parts, you know, family, friends, being good to other people—that stuff is universal. Plus, it's so commercialized these days, I'm happy to focus on people instead."

"Has it been lonely for you, because of your family?"

"It has. But once I became friends with Maria I got to hang out with her and her friends, and that helped a lot."

"She's really nice. Um. This might be too personal, but, um… You said that I was the third person besides your tattoo artist to see where your cat paw tattoo ended. Is Maria one of those three?"

"That *is* personal, but it's fine. Yes, she is one of the three. We, um, haven't dated in a long time, but, um, we have done the occasional friends with benefits thing."

"Wow. Um, okay. I'm not sure why I asked that. Sorry, I didn't mean to pry."

"It's okay, Megan. So anyway, when do you want to get a tree?"

"Maybe in a couple of weeks? I don't want to get it too early and have it all dry by Christmas, but not too late before all of the good ones are gone. Will it be okay with Nocturne?"

"I'm not sure, actually. She's never experienced a Christmas tree before. We'll at least do lights on the tree and maybe some wooden ornaments. Definitely no glass or tinsel. None of us want her pooping tinsel…"

"That makes sense. Um, about presents. Uh, I want to make sure that Sophia has a nice Christmas, but I'm not sure how much I'll have left over, especially after paying rent. We never discussed that before. How much should I contribute?"

"That's a lot. Maybe let's not worry about rent yet. You've been getting the groceries, so let's call it even for now."

"That doesn't sound fair to you."

"Megan, I can decide what's fair for me. Tell you what. Once you get settled down with PPS, let's sit down and figure out some kind of cost sharing. For right now, though, why don't you handle groceries and I'll handle rent, and we'll call it good, okay?"

"Alright, but only if you're sure."

"I'm sure. And don't worry about presents. Not between us, alright? You and Sophia being in my life, plus you getting me to talk with Momma again… You couldn't give me better presents than that. Plus, the holidays are stressful enough. We don't need to add to it by searching for gifts that neither of us needs."

"I like that, I like that a lot. Maybe we can find something to do, just us, or us and Sophia, as a gift to ourselves."

"The gift of an experience. That's perfect! Good idea, Megan! Since we're on the subject of gifts, though, I do want Sophia to get a nice gift from her Aunt Tasha. Do you have any thoughts about that?"

They discussed possible gifts for Sophia until dinner was ready. Then, after dinner, Sophia fed Nocturne, and they all spent time together as a family until it was time for Sophia to go to bed. Megan and Tasha did some late night yoga to clear out the kinks and stress of the week before getting ready for bed themselves.

CHAPTER 27

COLD SHOWER

Tasha woke up in a big pile of people, and, presumably, a cat. Sometime in the night, Sophia must have gotten up, because instead of being in the middle, she was on the outside, and Tasha was now in the middle. She could see Nocturne's ears, barely visible past Sophia. Meanwhile, she could feel Megan spooning her from behind. *Well, this is definitely different. I don't really have to get up anyway. I really hope that Megan moves her hand before she wakes up, because that is definitely going to be awkward otherwise.*

She was planning to work on some websites this morning for the adult boutiques that Lauren referred. Concentrating on this mental task list was more difficult than usual because she could feel the bare skin of Megan's legs touching hers. It was distracting.

It feels good, but it shouldn't feel good. Well, maybe it should feel good, but not this good. I haven't felt anyone touching me like this in a while. Maybe I should call Maria. Why does that somehow feel wrong now? Back to the websites. What was the one that I'm working on first? Uh, Playtime Princess or something. Okay, here's what I need to do...

Tasha continued mentally prioritizing and cataloging until Megan started snoring gently in her ear.

That's distracting.

Then Megan shifted, one of her legs sliding along Tasha's.

Yep, I gotta get up. I need coffee and a cold shower. A very cold shower.

Tasha managed to somehow extract herself without waking anyone except Nocturne. She started making coffee and then fed the desperately starving Nocturne, who was doing her best to convey the message that she had never been fed before and that Tasha needed to remedy this situation right now. Once that was done, Tasha grabbed yogurt and granola and sat down at her laptop. She was moving along productively when a bleary-eyed Megan stumbled out with a raging case of bedhead. Tasha watched her scratch her head and sniff the air.

Focus on work, girl.

"Coffee?"

"I made some a while ago. I think it's still hot."

"Awesome. Lemme pee." Megan turned toward the bathroom, absentmindedly scratching her butt. Tasha watched her walk away.

Why is this so hard? That's what she said! Ugh, grow up. She's your best friend, not some rando hook-up. Focus on setting up a sales page for vibrators. Oh, that's not helping right now. What do guys think of? Baseball? Focus on the work. It's boring and normal.

"Thanks for making coffee. You're the best. Whatcha workin' on? Oh, that's a lot of vibrators! That's gotta be fun to work on."

"Eh, it's not that much fun, really. Setting up a sales page for vibrators is basically the same as setting up a sales page for car parts or books." *I never realized that shirt was that loose before. And now I know that she doesn't wear a bra to sleep. Come on, Tasha. Get your shit together. Stop perving on your best friend.* "Um, did you sleep okay? Anything weird happen in the night?"

"I slept great. And weird how?"

"Uh, you know. Strange dreams or something?"

"No. Not that I remember. Did you have strange dreams?"

"No, just thought I'd ask. I want to make sure that you're okay." *Smooth. Real smooth recovery there, Tasha.*

"What are your plans for the day?"

"I want to do some freelance work this morning and then I'm taking Sophia to the cat shelter in the afternoon, to give you some time to yourself." *I desperately need some time to myself right now. Or maybe not just to myself. Oh good, now I have two internal monologues.* "What about you?"

"Well, as much as I appreciate the thought, I think that I'm going to go out to see if I can find some presents for Sophia. Thank you so much for taking her to the shelter. That really helps."

"My pleasure! I really enjoy spending time with her."

Tasha went back to her freelance work while Megan, gingerly cradling the mug of coffee in her hands, went to sit on the couch. They stayed like this until Sophia woke up and came out from the bedroom, accompanied by Nocturne. Megan got up and greeted her daughter, offering her breakfast. Nocturne meowed piteously, prompting Megan to offer her breakfast, too. Tasha broke out of her zone to inform Megan that Nocturne had already had breakfast that day, and that the meow was, in fact, a lie.

Once Sophia was fed, Tasha was vaguely aware of Megan asking her daughter to try doing yoga with her. The two changed clothes and got out the mats as Tasha continued to work. Tasha soon found herself observing them, watching Sophia try out the unfamiliar poses with the typical enthusiasm, erraticness, and flexibility of an eight-year-old. She then found her gaze drifting to the skintight yoga pants that Megan was borrowing, idly reflecting just how well they fit her friend's ass. *Really well. That is a very fine downward dog. If that shirt slides up any more... Get it together, girl. I really should have taken that cold shower.*

Tasha deliberately turned her laptop so that she could no longer see Megan and Sophia. She plugged in her headphones and put Prince on the playlist. The infectious grooves helped her focus on work, at least for a while. Then she realized that maybe Prince wasn't the best choice in her current state. "Raspberry Beret" quickly led Tasha's imagination to inappropriate places.

Tasha hit pause and desperately tried to think of anything that was catchy but not sexy. *Okay, time to listen to some Dio. If I get desperate, then there's always Pat Boone.* Tasha shuddered. *Come on, Ronnie James, don't make me listen to Pat Boone.* Tasha relaxed as "Stand Up and Shout" started playing, once again finding the zone, her fingers tapping wildly on the keyboard.

She had finished one project and was about halfway through the second when she felt a touch on her arm. Tasha hit pause and looked over her shoulder. "Hey, Megan what's up?"

"Um, I was going to ask if you want lunch, but now I'm thinking that I should probably also ask if maybe you could make sure that your laptop screen is facing in a way that Sophia won't see it." Megan pointed at the extremely large and anatomically accurate dildo currently on the screen. "I do realize that I need to have The Talk with Sophia at some point, probably sooner than I want, but maybe not this soon."

"Oh, yeah, sorry." *Also, sorry that I was perving on you so hard earlier that I had to turn away. Oh, by the way, you were getting a handful in your sleep.* "Lunch sounds good. Leftovers? And when you do have The Talk, I'm sure that some of Lauren's gifts would make great demonstration pieces," Tasha added mischievously.

"Thanks, Tasha… Now I'm terrified of her getting tall enough to reach the high shelves in the closet."

"You're welcome! That's what friends are for." Tasha grinned at her.

As Megan pulled leftover scampi out of the fridge, she said, "It looked like you were rocking out."

"Yeah, some Dio-era Black Sabbath."

"I think I've only listened to the original line-up."

"Those Ozzy-era albums were awesome. Here, listen to this." Tasha pulled out the headphones and hit play. "This is the title track of the *Heaven and Hell* album."

"Oh, my god… that bass line. Wow. I'll have to check that out later. Sophia, come join us for lunch, sweetie."

After lunch, Tasha took Sophia to the cat shelter for a few

hours while Megan went out to find presents for Sophia. Tasha texted to make sure that Megan was home and that the presents were well hidden before returning. Once home, she and Sophia changed clothes to keep from spreading anything to Nocturne. Tasha then showed Megan and Sophia how to make samosas.

All in all, it was a very pleasant day for all three of them. Once Sophia was in bed, Tasha went back to work, hoping to finish before she went to sleep. She felt in the mood for some sleazy-good rock and roll. *Hmmm, AC/DC? Crüe? KISS would work. Oh, there. Kix it is.* Tasha kept working until Megan headed to bed. Eventually, she laid down to sleep on the couch. *How do I tell her that I am sleeping out here because I'm thinking really inappropriate things about her?*

CHAPTER 28
SWITCH 625

Megan didn't sleep well that night. She still hadn't decided if she was going to take Tasha up on her offer to meet with Brad on Sunday afternoon. Worrying about that meeting made it hard to even get to sleep, and then she didn't sleep well. Sophia sleeping next to her was a comfort. She had grown accustomed to Tasha sleeping in the bed with the two of them, but for some reason Tasha had never come to bed, so now that was worrying her, too. Once she did finally wake up on Sunday morning, Megan did not feel well-rested at all.

As she headed for the bathroom, Megan saw Tasha sitting on the couch, apparently working. Not smelling coffee, her next move once she was finished would be to start that. *Weird. Whoever is up first always starts on coffee. Maybe Tasha is planning to go out for coffee? I should check on that first.*

Megan sat down on the arm of the couch and said, "Good morning, Tasha. Do you want me to make coffee, or are you going out for some?"

"Oh, I forgot. If you could make some, that would be great."

No eye contact. I hope she's not sick or something. "You didn't pull an all-nighter, did you?"

"No, I was just too tired to move, so I slept on the couch."

"How did you sleep?"

"Meh, it wasn't great. Now I'm working on the last freelance project."

"I didn't sleep well, either. This meeting with Brad has me really wound up."

"I get that."

Megan sat down on the couch and watched as Tasha shifted away from her. "I'm sorry. You're working and here I am interrupting you."

Tasha looked up. "Hey, no. I'm sorry. I'm just… I'm just feeling off."

"Are you sick?"

"No, it's not that. Physically I feel fine."

"Are we crowding you? You're used to living on your own and now there are two other people living with you. We're all practically on top of each other." Tasha made a strange face at that last sentence. Megan thought her expression looked like a combination of embarrassment and humor. "I can start looking for a new place."

"No! Megan, it's… it's not that. I really like having you and Sophia here. You're right that I'm used to living alone, but I feel like this change has been so good for me. I think that maybe I'm struggling a bit to adjust to the new circumstances, but that's a good thing. I just need to adjust a bit more and everything will be fine. I promise. Plus, work has been a grind."

Megan wasn't entirely convinced, but she didn't want to press things. Instead, she changed the subject. "Does your offer to meet Brad still stand?"

"Of course!"

"Thank you. I'm already worried about being too trusting, and feeling as tired as I do… I don't think it's a good idea."

"I've got you."

"Hey, don't feel like you have to. I can call him and reschedule. He'd probably rather watch football anyway."

"Megan, it's fine. I'll meet with him today."

"Okay, thank you. I have some stuff to go over with you, but that can wait until you're done. Lemme check on the coffee. I'll be back in a minute with yours if it's ready, then I'll leave you alone. Oh, I'll feed Nocturne too so that you can focus."

"Thanks, Megan."

CHAPTER 29

EVERY ROSE HAS ITS THORN

Brad arrived a few minutes early to one of Portland's many brew pubs and found a fairly isolated table. He thought about having a beer but decided that, as much as he would probably need one after this, soda would be the better option. Last Saturday had been an abject disaster and he wasn't optimistic about today. His father had been extremely disappointed at his failure and had buried him in punishment projects at work this past week. He had no idea how to handle that situation. In fact, he felt completely out of his depth in every facet of his life.

Brad didn't feel any better when he saw Tasha walk in with two envelopes in her hand. Legal-sized envelopes. He had spent enough years in the banking world to know that almost anything in a legal-sized envelope was serious. The fact that it was Tasha and not Megan holding them meant nothing good for him, he was sure. She frowned when she saw him and stalked over.

"Hi, Tasha," he said, forcing himself to be as pleasant as possible.

"Brad," she said, taking a seat and tossing the envelopes on the table.

"Where's Megan?"

"She's taking Sophia to roller derby. She also knows that she's fallen for your bullshit way too many times. So now you get me instead."

"Uh huh. What's in the envelopes?"

"We're not talking about that right now, Brad," Tasha said his name with immense distaste.

Brad stayed silent, assuming that speaking was probably not going to do him any good. "You came into my home… into *our* home… and said some damn stupid things, Brad." He wisely kept his mouth shut.

"You and I, we never liked each other much. Not at first, and not now. But one thing that I never thought was that you were stupid. An over-privileged White boy riding Daddy's coattails for sure, but not stupid. Holy shit, though. You got deep in the stupid, didn't you?"

"I could have handled that better."

"No shit!" Tasha snorted. "I gotta ask. What the hell were you thinking?"

"I don't know."

"And we're back to stupid again. Of course you knew. I know you didn't drive all that way, thinking that you'd show up and Megan would just go home with you."

Brad really couldn't think of a good response.

"Oh, shit. That *actually was* your plan! Wasn't it? Again, what the hell were you thinking?"

"I don't know, Tasha. I wasn't. I showed up at Thanksgiving without Megan and Sophia and my dad read me the riot act. He told me that I was weak and that I needed to be a man. He said that Megan needed a strong man to tell her what to do. He said that if I didn't go get her then everyone would know what a pussy I am. He said, 'You're a pussy, Brad, and everyone knows what happens to pussies.' So, I tried to do what Dad would do."

"Your dad is an asshole, Brad. I mean, you should never, ever take his advice. Especially about women. Megan's not some pushover that you can just order around. You didn't do that shit while you were married, did you?" Tasha's voice was rising.

"No! I mean, we argued and stuff, but it wasn't like that. I guess I was just so desperate and humiliated that I did something stupid."

"That there is a start, Brad. What was that other bullshit?"

"Um. I—"

"Come on. I know that you weren't that ignorant back in college, so you musta learned it somewhere along the way."

"I got on some message boards in the past few years. Lots of guys talking about how we don't learn real history in school."

"Lemme guess, these assholes knew the 'real history.'" Tasha's air quotes at the end were practically dripping with disdain.

"Yeah, I, um, maybe should have been more discerning."

"Oh… Ya think?!? Tell you what. We don't learn the real history in school, because the real history is awful and a whole bunch of White folk don't want their kids learning how evil their great-granddaddy was." Tasha's native South Carolinian accent was starting to show.

Brad nodded and kept his mouth shut.

"I could do this all day, but I'd rather not." Tasha tapped the two envelopes. "Let's talk about why you're here and why I'm here, because I'd rather be anywhere else. Megan's divorcing you, Brad." She spread the two envelopes apart. "What happens now depends on you and me. Megan, bless her wonderful heart, wants you to be part of Sophia's life. She wants Sophia to have a good father. Someone that she can love and trust as she grows up. Personally, I think that you're a pile of shit and that you'll always be a pile of shit. That's why there are two envelopes. See, Megan doesn't trust you, and we all know why, but you've fooled her before. You've never fooled me, Brad."

"So, I have to convince you that I'm not a pile of shit. If I do that, then I get the good envelope. If I don't, then I get the bad envelope."

"I mean, you're never going to convince me that you aren't a pile of shit who cheated on my best friend at least twice, but maybe you can convince me that you can change."

"I'm not sure how I can do that. You already hate me. With reason."

"You're right. Megan gave me a bunch of questions to ask, and I'll use a bit of that, but really, we're doing things my way. I have a list. Think of it like the labors of Hercules, except not nearly as heroic. Now, which envelope would you like?"

Brad wasn't feeling optimistic. This hadn't gone well, but it could have been much worse. He worried that "worse" was coming real soon.

"I'd definitely prefer the good one."

"Good choice. First, I'm gonna give you a couple of books to read. You're going to read them and then send me a book report, and that better be an A+++ book report. I'm gonna write them on the good envelope. Lemme make sure that I get this 100% correct for you." She whipped out her phone. "*Caste: The Origins of Our Discontents*, by Isabel Wilkerson and *The Half Has Never Been Told: Slavery and the Making of American Capitalism* by Edward Baptist. I am putting my email address on there, too. I expect your first book report in my inbox next weekend."

"Yes, I can do that."

"That wasn't on Megan's list, but I'm here and you pissed me off, so it's on the list now. I'm glad to hear that you'll do that. Next item. Based on Megan's questions, you aren't vaccinated for COVID. Is that right?"

"Yes."

"What the hell, Brad. Really. Get the damn shot."

"I've done all this research—"

"Brad, you ain't done shit. You went on Google and typed in words. Actual research involves highly educated and trained scientists running tightly monitored experiments with control groups, and then other groups of highly educated and trained scientists successfully replicating the work of the first group. Did you do any of that, Brad?"

"No."

"Did you just type some shit into Google?"

"Yes. But those scientists are all getting paid by big pharmaceutical companies."

"Not the government ones, Brad, and so help me, if you say one thing about the Deep State or a globalist cabal, you will absolutely get the bad envelope right now."

Brad wisely kept his mouth shut.

"And of course the drug companies are making shitloads of money off this. Jesus, Brad, you're a banker. Your entire job is to suck on the teats of capitalism. This is America. Nothing gets done to benefit regular folk if billionaires can't find a way to make money off of it."

Brad actually agreed with that last point, even if it sounded vaguely progressive.

"Here's what you're going to do." Tasha gave him a hard look. "You're going to get the shots, and I want proof. If you send me a fake vax card, then you will get the bad envelope."

"I'll do it, I swear."

I might have to come back to Portland to get vaccinated. I don't need my neighbors knowing that I got "the jab." That's as bad as wearing a mask back home.

"Next, you're gonna stop banging homewrecking skanks."

"I can do that."

"I mean it, Brad. What if that had been Sophia walking in on you banging what's her name?"

"Margar—"

"I don't need her name, Brad."

"I'm done with her, I swear."

"It's not just her, Brad. It's you. You're also a homewrecking skank. Maybe you find someone, maybe you don't. I honestly don't care. You need to promise me that when you go out with someone, the top priority in your mind is, 'would Sophia be proud of my choices.'"

Brad realized that a lot hinged on this moment. He looked Tasha squarely in the eyes and said, "I will do my absolute best to be the father that Sophia can be proud of and to make good choices in whoever I date. And if I realize that I made a mistake or find out something that would not make Sophia proud of me, then I will own up to my failures and learn from them."

"Wow, Brad. That was very nicely done. I almost believe you. Next, you need to find a new church. There's plenty of options available in Christianity. Find one that doesn't hate gay people, because if they hate one group, chances are that they'll get around to hating more."

I don't think that there are any other options where I live. I'll figure something out. Heck, I can just stay home and read the Bible.

"Uh, I can do that."

They went on from there, but Brad felt that the skanks question was the tipping point.

A few minutes later, Tasha said, "I can't believe that I'm doing this, but here's the good envelope. Now, don't think that you're in the clear yet. If you screw this up, I'm very happy to give you the bad envelope."

"Thank you, Tasha." He opened the envelope and skimmed through the divorce papers.

The offer seemed surprisingly generous. "I'll have to have my lawyer take a look at this, but it seems acceptable."

"You do that." Tasha stood up to leave.

"Tasha, wait. Back in school, why didn't you like me?"

"Honestly?"

"Please."

"Because I know you, Brad. Because I grew up with dozens of guys just like you. Wealthy family with connections. Over-privileged and arrogant. Convinced that their shit don't stink and never, ever having to deal with real consequences. My folks sent me to one of the elite Christian schools, never mind that it started out as a segregation academy."

"What's that?"

"After Brown and then the Civil Rights Act, White folks couldn't keep kids like me out of their public schools, so suddenly a whole bunch of private Christian schools opened up. A lot of them were in the South, but they were everywhere. Eventually, they lost their tax exempt status unless they started accepting Black kids. So, I was one of a handful of Black kids in a sea of White kids. We had to be *exceptional*. Perfect grades and damn good at sports, too. Dante played basketball and I played soccer. All-state, both of us. Meanwhile, Thaddeus Moneybags IV didn't have to be good at shit. Guys like that could screw around, do drugs, whatever. Well, coke and weed. Heroin was apparently un-Christian. Oh yeah, I got asked for drugs all the time."

"Really, why?"

"Because I'm Black. They figured that since I'm Black that I must have a dozen dealers on speed dial."

"Are you sure?"

"Brad, don't make me give you the bad envelope. Of course I'm sure. I know because at least once a month, some stoner would come up to me and say something like, 'Hey, my boys and I are going camping this weekend and need some killer bud, can you hook a brother up?' and then I'd nicely tell them no because if I told them to fuck off like I wanted to then I might get expelled. Then they'd say, 'We really need those dank buds, can you hook us up with one of your homies?' So, yeah, it was because I'm Black. They did the same shit to Dante."

"Wow, I'm sorry."

"And then you come rolling into Megan's life. I told her that you were a dipshit, but she didn't listen. I was right, too. She's better than you. She's always been better than you. And she deserves more than you. She deserves everything."

"Oh, shit."

"What?"

"You're in love with her!"

"What? No!"

Brad watched Tasha's face as her mind spun. He now knew why she had never liked him and suddenly, he realized why he had never liked her. Jealousy. He had always been jealous of Tasha. *Well, ain't that a kick in the nuts.*

Tasha stood and grabbed her coat. "I gotta go!" With that, she was running for the door.

CHAPTER 30
LISTEN TO YOUR HEART

Tasha's mind was whirling furiously. *Oh shit, oh shit, oh shit. How did I not see this? How the hell did Brad see this? Brad? I'm so screwed. I have to tell her. I can't tell her. She's straight, I'm… whatever… not straight. This could ruin everything. This will ruin everything. Maybe it won't ruin everything. She's my friend, she'll be cool. Sure, she'll be cool when you tell her that you love her and want to spend the rest of your lives together. That'll be totally fine. Wait, the rest of our lives, where did that come from? This will definitely ruin everything.*

Not knowing what to do, Tasha panicked and picked up her phone. "Hello, dear," Maria said as she answered Tasha's call.

"Maria, I'm so glad that you picked up! I'm in trouble."

"You didn't murder Brad, did you?"

"No—I love Megan!"

"I know, dear."

"Wait, what?"

"It's obvious. Well, obvious to everyone except you two."

"I don't understand."

"Did you ever wonder why we never worked out?"

"Uh, yeah, a bit."

"I love you dearly, Tasha, but you were already taken. I didn't know her name then. I didn't even know that this mystery person was a woman. I just could never compare to Megan, even if you didn't know that you were making that comparison."

"I'm sorry, Maria. I… I didn't know."

"It's quite alright, Tasha. I would have never been able to give you what you truly need, and quite frankly, I enjoy my freedom too much anyway. You are a one woman kind of girl, and I am very definitely not. We've had our fun, though, although I suspect that time has now come to a close."

"What do I do now? I can't tell her. I'll ruin everything!" Tasha was fighting back tears by this point.

"My one rule, the most important rule—there are no secrets between loved ones."

"I can't! I can't risk it!"

"Tasha. Dear. Do you truly love Megan?"

She wiped away her tears and sniffled. "Yes."

"Would you be heartbroken if she found another? Let's say, another Brad?"

Tasha sobbed. "Yes! But I would support her, of course."

"Of course you would, because you are amazing. And yet, this is why you must risk everything and tell her. You love her, you can't stomach the idea of living without her, and yet you would do just that if it would make her happy. For your sake, for Megan's sake, you must take this leap of faith. Trust. In. Love."

"I will tell her, Maria. Tomorrow. I promise."

"No, dear. No secrets between loved ones. Tell her today. And Tasha?"

"Yes?"

"Once you tell her, accept her immediate reaction and be prepared to be patient. She truly loves you, she doesn't know it yet."

"How can you be sure?"

"I watched you both at Friendsgiving. You both kept such a close eye on Sophia, yet you also kept a close eye on each other. Megan was quite nervous, you know. Among strangers, uncomfortable in that magnificent dress, and yet, whenever she struggled, you were there. She reacted, she responded to you, Tasha. She trusts you completely."

"I… I didn't know."

"As I said, your love is only a mystery to the two of you."

"I'll tell her, Maria."

"Do it today. If not today, then Wednesday."

"Wednesday? Why Wednesday?"

"Some of us started a betting pool on when you two would admit that you love each other. Wednesday is the date I picked, dear."

Tasha was speechless.

"Goodbye, dear. And remember what I said." Maria hung up.

Tasha walked home. It was a longish walk, but she needed to clear her head. Night was coming by the time she got home, and Megan and Sophia were already there.

"Tasha! You're back. Is everything alright?"

"Hi, Aunt Tasha! Roller derby is so much fun! I really want to play. Tell Mommy that it's okay for me to play."

"Hello, munchkin. I'm glad that you had fun. I promise to talk to your mom for you."

"I'm right here…"

"She's just being protective. You're her little angel, and moms get worried. It's their job."

"I know," Sophia responded in that classic high-low of a child who hasn't gotten their way (yet?).

"But Aunt Tasha, she's the fun aunt, so she's going to do everything that she can to convince your mom, right?"

"Yay!"

"I'm still right here…"

"Hey, you." Tasha smiled at Megan. "Um, we need to talk."

"We do, how did things go? Which envelope did you give him?"

"Oh, that. It went well, actually. I still can't believe it, but I gave him the good one."

"Really? I wasn't expecting that. It must have taken forever if you're just getting home now."

"Oh, no, I was done hours ago. I walked home."

"Why?"

"I needed to think." Tasha held up her hand before Megan could ask anything else.

"Okay, Megan, stop with the questions. I have to tell you something. It's important."

"Oh, okay."

"Megan, I love you."

"Tasha, I love you, too."

"No, Megan." Tasha's heart raced, she felt the sweat on her palms as she took Megan's hand in her own, looked her in the eyes, and leapt. "I. Love. You."

She saw Megan's eyes widen as her words sunk in. She heard Megan utter a long, "Oooohhhh." She saw the fear. She saw the uncertainty. Her heart shattered. And then Megan's arms were around her, holding her up. Tasha felt like her entire world was imploding, and then Megan whispered in her ear. "Tasha, thank you for telling me. Please, just give me some time. I... I just need a little time."

Tasha remembered Maria's words from earlier. To accept. To be patient. To trust. "Of course, Megan. Take whatever time you need. I trust you."

CHAPTER 31
HEAVEN AND HELL

Tasha's confession… profession… of love had thrown Megan for a loop. Thankfully, at eight, Sophia was generally self-sufficient and if she did need anything that afternoon, then Tasha stepped in seamlessly. Tasha. *Tasha loves me. Not as friends, or maybe as friends but also more. And my reaction was to ask her to let me think about it? What the hell, Megan. It's a wonder that she's still here. Hell, it's her apartment, it's a wonder that I'm still here!*

Hours later, even after a long walk, Megan's mind was still in chaos. One thing was becoming clear to her. She needed to say something to Tasha. Megan felt that this was about to be the hardest conversation of her life. Sophia was reading on the couch, absentmindedly stroking a sleeping Nocturne. Tasha was puttering around the kitchen as Megan walked up to her. "Can we talk?"

"Are you ready now?" Megan couldn't help but notice a slightly bitter undertone in Tasha's voice, yet mixed with hope.

"No, but yes. Maybe in the bedroom?"

"Fine."

They both sat down on the bed. Megan took a deep breath, which did little to calm her racing nerves. "Thank you, Tasha, for telling me how you feel. I know that must have been difficult, and you are incredibly brave. I also feel like I hurt you deeply. I'm sorry. I'm a mess right now, and yet you still love me. I love you, too, Tasha. With all of my heart."

She watched the fear drain away from Tasha's face, replaced by joy. Megan continued before Tasha could respond, "And I'm terrified. I'm terrified that this could be a rebound, and I'll end up hurting you. I'm terrified about the possibility of loving another woman. Sophia loves you, and I'm terrified that I'm going to fuck this up and hurt both of you."

Tasha silently rose up and then sat down again, right next to Megan, and took her in her arms. Megan rested her head on Tasha's collarbone and started to cry. "I love you, Tasha. It feels overwhelming, but I don't know how to love you… as a woman, and I don't ever want to lose you."

"You won't lose me, Megan. We'll figure this out, okay?"

Megan nodded, but she wasn't okay. She was definitely a mess. She felt like a coward for taking the safe choices for most of her life. She felt brave for telling Tasha that she loved her. She hadn't lied to Tasha when she said that she was terrified, because she was. Megan was in wholly uncharted territory, and what she wanted to do most in this moment was run. She held onto Tasha with both arms, hoping that this feeling would pass and that she wouldn't want to run anymore.

Megan's panic slowly subsided, as did her tears. Even so, she could feel a vast well of anxiety inside of her.

I'm going to hurt her. I just know it, and I can't bear to think about it. I need to talk to someone, and she's the only person that I trust. She is also the one person that I can't talk to about this. I love her so much it hurts.

Megan went to bed shortly after Sophia. She was emotionally wiped out. Before going to bed, she said, "Tasha, please sleep in the bed tonight. It's better when you're there."

CHAPTER 32
A NEW ATTITUDE

Tasha woke up on Monday feeling amazing. Yesterday was an emotional roller coaster, but she felt good about where she and Megan were. Yes, Megan was having some challenges, but they loved each other and would figure it out together. As the trio got ready for Monday, Tasha relished every touch, every smile. She practically skipped as she took Sophia to school. Not even Kevin could break her spirit today. Feeling mischievous and remembering her promise to Maria, Tasha brought her red dress to work, planning to surprise Megan with it at the holiday party on Friday.

Some managers see someone feeling cheerful and then try to spread that feeling to infect the whole team, creating a warm and open work environment. Kevin believed that he was one of those managers, but he wasn't. His reward for Tasha being in a good mood was to pile a ton of work into her inbox. She plugged in some disco and Motown and just grooved through it.

Tasha divided her work into two different categories. There was work for clients, which was occasionally interesting and was at least productive. Then there were projects for Kevin, which were basically a waste of time. She knew this because Javier, whom she shared a cubicle wall with, admitted that he had been letting an AI program do his reports since spring, and Kevin hadn't noticed. He'd actually been praised for the quality of his reports. So now Tasha let an AI do much of the work for Kevin, although she always checked to make sure it didn't do anything too crazy.

At lunch, Tasha checked her personal email and saw a message from Lauren. Lauren was very pleased at the increased web traffic from Tasha's changes to the website. She also told Tasha to keep an eye on her personal emails as more freelance work was coming her way. Tasha responded with a quick email to thank her.

This isn't a bad side gig. Maybe I can make enough doing websites for women-owned adult boutiques that I can afford insurance and rent and can quit this job. Probably not, but I can dream.

During the afternoon, she received four emails from four different businesses asking for her assistance with website redesigns. Interestingly, none of the four were adult boutiques and all wanted her help with apps as well. She was done with her work, but Kevin didn't know that, so she spent the time discussing wants and needs for these potential clients, as well as timeframes. She was going to be busy, but that was okay. Eventually one of her clients sent in a request, so she went back to her actual job.

She always made sure to keep an eye out, though. Kevin liked to take a stroll around the office every day. He called it "taking a break from meetings." No one was ever sure why he had so many meetings or what was discussed. The speculation about Kevin's meetings was probably the biggest topic of conversation for Tasha and her co-workers. Sometimes his strolls interrupted their work, which was annoying. Other times, he interrupted whatever they were doing to make it look like they were working. Tasha wasn't sure which was worse.

Tasha finished her work for the client a little after five and then whiled away the last few minutes looking at the furbabies channel on Slack. Her bus ride home wasn't that long, but it seemed to drag on forever. She practically bounced through the door. Megan was finishing dinner and Sophia was feeding Nocturne. After dinner, she and Megan did some yoga. Tonight, Sophia even joined them.

Relaxed and even-keeled after yoga, Tasha reflected on her day and, as she did, cracks started to emerge in her new attitude. Little things that she had ignored suddenly surfaced in her mind. How Megan's laughter had sounded a bit forced. How Tasha had touched Megan, but she couldn't remember Megan touching her. Was something wrong? She knew that Megan was trying to adjust to their newly expressed feelings, but was she having cold feet?

Now Tasha was starting to worry, but she didn't know how to express that. Especially to Megan.

CHAPTER 33
UNDER PRESSURE

Megan noticed a shift in Tasha's mood on Tuesday morning. She had tried very hard since their talk on Sunday to be super positive around Tasha, but she must be doing something wrong. Possibly a lot of wrong if Tasha had gone from elated to withdrawn so quickly.

'Fake it 'til you make it' isn't working. What am I going to do? Stay positive and smile. It will be alright! It's not going to be alright. Breathe, girl.

"Do you want to have a movie night tonight?" Tasha asked.

"Yeah, that would be fun."

"Maybe one of those Hallmark or Lifetime holiday rom-coms that you seem to like so much."

"Yeah, that would be great."

"It's a date, then!"

They were both forcing enthusiasm, and Megan felt like neither of them was convincing the other. "Hey, Tasha. We got this, okay?"

"Yeah, thanks, Megan."

"Do you want anything special for our movie date? Popcorn, pizza, candy?"

"Uh, anything is fine. You pick."

"Okay, I'll surprise you."

This is awful. We have all the energy of two middle-schoolers being forced to read a passage from Shakespeare in class. What is wrong with us? You know, besides me. I'm sabotaging this and I don't know why. I want this! It's like Estelle and John talked about, I can't imagine my life without Tasha and yet somehow I can't seem to show that.

The vast well of anxiety that Megan felt inside of her was straining to get out. She could feel the panic starting to build, the hairs on the back of her neck beginning to rise. "I, uh… I forgot that I need to go in a bit early today. You're still alright with walking Sophia to school, right?"

"Yeah, I got her."

"Okay, thanks!"

And now I'm running like a coward. Oh, and abandoning my daughter as well. That's just great, Megan. You're really hitting every mark today, aren't you?

She drove to school and then sat in her car, crying for a good ten minutes.

Get your shit together, Megan. You are a professional and you're going to get through this school day. You might be a wreck on the inside, but these kids are never going to know that, are they? That, at least, you can do. Then you are going to go home and be with your daughter and your best friend.

Megan held it together at school that day. As she got in her car, her phone rang.

And here's the cherry on the shit sundae that is my life right now.

"Hi, Brad."

"Hi, Megan. Um, please tell Tasha that I started the reading that she wanted me to do. I'll get her the reports soon."

The what? Did she give him homework? What reports? What the hell?

"Uh, sure, Brad. I'll tell her."

"Thanks."

"That can't be the reason that you called."

"Oh… No, it isn't. On Sunday, Tasha mentioned that you took

Sophia to… roller derby, I think she said. That sounds dangerous for an eight-year-old."

"Yes, we went to roller derby, but she isn't playing it. Not yet, at least. She wants to, though. I actually wanted to talk with you about that before I signed her up or anything."

"I'm not sure about this."

"Brad, what do you know about roller derby?"

"My dad used to talk about watching it in the 70s. Lots of fights and stuff."

"I don't know about that, but this is very different. It's a real sport and there are no fights. For kids Sophia's age, there are apparently limited contact rules too."

"Huh, that doesn't sound so bad. What team is this?"

"It's a league here in Portland for adults and juniors. Rose City Rollers. Why?"

"I want to see their website. What's this about Wreckers?"

"That's their recreational league for adult skaters."

"Ohhhh… Wreckers, recreational… I get it."

"Of course *you* like the pun."

"There's a juniors championship in a couple weekends. I'd like to come and see it for myself."

"What? Really?"

"Yes. You and your hired muscle have made it clear that I need to get my shit together. So, this is me trying to get my shit together for my… for *our* daughter's sake."

"Don't think that this changes how I feel about you."

"I know. According to Tasha I'm a big pile of shit. I have the divorce papers. Really though, if Sophia is interested in watching or playing roller derby, then I want to learn about it, too."

"What the hell did Tasha say to you, Brad?"

"Let's just say that it was a learning opportunity for me."

"Huh. Look, Brad. Sophia wants this really badly. I think that it could be really good for her, too."

"I'll keep that in mind. So, is it alright for me to see this with you two Sundays from now?"

"With us? I mean, I encourage you to come and see it. I'm not sure how I feel about you being with us, though. I will think about it."

"Okay, I get that. I do want to spend some time with her, if possible. I miss her. I also want to experience her interest and find out what she likes about roller derby, if that makes sense."

"It does. I'll think about it and then get back to you."

"Thanks Megan."

"Sure, Brad. Bye."

Tasha must have put the fear of God into him. She is fierce. And confident. If I had half of her confidence then maybe I wouldn't be in this mess with her.

CHAPTER 34

IT'S ALL COMING BACK TO ME NOW

The next two days were rough on everyone. Megan and Tasha continued to simmer in their own fears and resentments. Sophia picked up on their mood and got feisty. Even Nocturne was getting hissy. No one was happy.

Tasha waited until Sophia was in bed on Thursday night, a process that involved shouting by both Megan and Sophia. Once Sophia was down, she said quietly, "We need to talk."

Possibly the deadliest four words in the English language. Whenever someone says "we need to talk" it's rarely a good thing.

Megan said, "I know."

"I want to start by saying thank you. I spent too many years not speaking with Momma because of stupid pride. You helped me get over that and I'm forever grateful. So, I'm not going to make the same mistake twice. Megan, this isn't working and I don't know why."

"It's all my fault! I'm trying my best, but I can't seem to do anything right. Um, I'm so sorry. I knew I would ruin everything. We'll move out this weekend, I promise."

"No! Megan... I love you. You're not moving out, okay? I

know that you're trying really hard. Maybe you're trying too hard."

"I just want to be perfect for you."

"Megan, you don't have to be perfect, you just have to be you. I want to tell you something."

"Okay."

"On Sunday, when I talked with Maria, she said something to me. Well, first, she asked if I knew why she and I never worked out and then she said it was because I was already taken."

"What does that mean?"

"It means I was already in love with you, I just didn't realize it yet. I've thought a lot about that since then, and I believe that Maria's right. Even going back to college, no one was ever good enough, because no one was you."

"But what if I'm not good enough for you, either?"

"You are, Megan! Remember the past few weeks, how much fun we had, how easy things were? Then we both said 'I love you' and everything went to shit. Maybe we should try to worry less about that and just be who we are?"

"I'd like that. I feel like I've been trying so hard, and that has made you anxious, which makes me anxious. Now I just have to figure out how to be natural. I'm really in my head about this, aren't I?"

"Yeah, you seem to be having trouble getting out of your own way. If I'm being honest, I think I am, too. Like… I told you that I love you and I just expected fireworks. It's okay that there weren't fireworks. You needed to process that, but I feel like I just want to skip past all the hard stuff and get to 'I do.'"

"Wait, what?"

"Oh, shit, I'm sorry!"

"No, Tasha, it's okay, really. Thank you, that's amazing. I'm still married to Brad and getting a divorce and you're thinking that you want us to say 'I do' and that's a lot. I mean, I'm a little bit leery about marriage right now, because… you know. But, you are amazing and you are definitely not Brad. Um… am I making any sense?"

"Sort of."

"Tasha, I'm really really not ready for 'I do' right now. I may never be ready, and that's not because of you. That's because of me. I tell you what, um… thank you for being honest with me, that means a lot."

"Of course!"

"And… if I ever feel like I *am* ready to get married again, then I'm buying the ring and I'm proposing. That's the deal."

"Can I ask why?"

"When Brad proposed, even for all that happened afterward, it was kind of magical in its own way. I mean, if I could go back in time, tell him absolutely not, and yet still have Sophia, then I would totally do that. Sorry, what I'm saying is, I've already had that moment and I want you to have it, too. If that makes sense."

"Megan, that's so sweet! I like your idea, but maybe we could think about proposing to each other at the same time. I'd really like to give you that magic as well, but, you know, without having to remember Brad."

"Well, like I said, I'm not sure if I'm ready, and, you know, still getting divorced, but yes, let's talk. I mean, we should talk about everything."

"Yes, we should. Hey, Megan."

"Yes, Tasha."

"We're talking and sharing right now, and I don't feel whatever weird vibe we've had all week. Do you?"

"No, actually, this is really nice. Like we're just communicating and not trying. And… now I might be overthinking things again."

"It's fine. I'm just glad that we could talk again. I feel so much better now."

"Me too. We should probably get to bed soon. We're still going to your work party tomorrow, right?"

"Yeah, if you want to. Really, don't feel like you have to."

"No, it'll be fun. And if it isn't, then Maria is watching Sophia and we can have a girls night."

"Oh, good call, Megan!"

"Thanks!" Megan grinned at her. "Oh, is there a dress code or anything?"

"Nah, casual," Tasha said, thinking of her red dress and surprising Megan.

CHAPTER 35
ONE NIGHT IN BANGKOK

Maria eagerly awaited Megan and Sophia's arrival. She knew that she only had about two hours to implement her plan, so the timing was not ideal, but she knew that she could make this work.

Oh, this is going to be delightful! I hope that Megan doesn't put up too much of a fuss, though. Any delay could throw everything off.

Thankfully, Megan was punctual. Maria watched as she parked and bundled Sophia out of the car. She opened the door as they approached. "Sophia! Megan! Welcome! It is lovely to see you both again."

"Hi, Maria!" Sophia said.

"Thank you for watching Sophia," Megan said. "It's very kind of you."

"It's my pleasure! It will be nice for you and Tasha to have a girls night. I'm sure that Sophia and I will have a wonderful time."

"I hope so. Sophia, thank Ms. Rodriguez for watching you."

"Thank you, Ms. Rodriguez!"

"You are quite welcome, Sophia. I see that your mom brought some books and games. I do like games! Maybe you can teach me one!" *Meanwhile, it's time to set my own little game in motion.* Maria turned to Megan. "Are you planning to wear that, dear?"

"Oh, this?" Megan surveyed her jeans, blouse, and cardigan. "Tasha said that it was a casual event."

"It is a holiday party, and that is definitely more 'working mom' than festive." *And now to set the hook.* "Hmm, I think that I have just the thing for you."

"Uh, that's okay, Maria. Maybe I should just run home and change. I have plenty of time to do that."

"No, I won't hear of it. Come along." With that, Maria strode off, heading for the staircase. She'd long ago realized that confidence and the unspoken assumption that someone will do as asked often led to them doing as asked. As Maria expected, Megan and Sophia followed along in her wake. Once upstairs, she led them to a well-lit guest bedroom.

As Megan entered, she saw the other people in the room and stiffened. "Maria, what's going on?" she asked warily.

"It's a surprise for you, my dear! I felt that you deserved something special for your first evening out alone with Tasha, so I brought in some friends to help. Just sit in that chair and these ladies will get you ready for a night out!"

"This is too much, Maria!"

"Nonsense, Megan. Their last show just wrapped, so we're helping them with a bit of holiday bonus cash, and you'll look stunning."

"Show?"

"Yes, Portland is much cheaper than Los Angeles, so we often get TV shows and movies filming here. Now you'll get the same hair and make-up treatment as the stars!"

"I can't!"

"Of course you can! Sophia and I will be right over here playing a game while you sit back and relax and let them work their movie magic on you." Maria turned to Sophia. "It will be fun to watch your mom get made up like a movie star, won't it, Sophia?"

"Yes, Ms. Rodriguez!"

"See, Megan. Just relax and let them work."

Megan didn't look sure, but she was ushered into the chair and then surrounded by a flurry of activity. After about thirty minutes, Maria called a halt to the proceedings.

"Before you get too far, this Hollywood look needs something more. Megan, go into the closet there. I believe that's where you will find your dress."

"Maria, what? This is fine."

"Trust me, the mom look is wonderful for a teacher, but you need to up your game tonight."

Megan reluctantly stood up and went into the closet. "Holy shit! Maria, get in here right now." The anger in her voice brooked no argument.

"Forgive me a moment, Sophia. I must tend to your mother." With that, Maria glided to the closet and entered. "What's wrong, Megan?"

"What's wrong?" Megan hissed. "This dress probably costs more than I make in a year! I can't wear this!"

"Oh, it assuredly does, dear. It's my gift to you."

"Gift? Why? Hell, we never even talked about your fees for my divorce."

"As to why, it is because Tasha loves you, and you love her back."

"She told you?"

"She called me in a panic last Sunday and told me that she loved you. I trust that she told you that. You haven't run off and are in fact going to a holiday party with her, which tells me that you reciprocate her feelings." Maria enjoyed Megan's shocked look. "As to my fees, I am the preferred divorce lawyer for the soon-to-be ex-wives of hedge fund bros and tech billionaires. Women who supported their husbands, raised families, and then were discarded for a younger model. I don't charge much, but when the payout is that many millions, well, let's just say that I don't really need to work ever again. But I carry on because I do so enjoy ripping their cheating balls off. But you, Megan, have brought joy to Tasha's life, and that is payment enough. Besides, what's the point of being rich if you can't make people's lives better?"

"I… I don't know what to say."

"Say yes to the dress, or whatever that saying is. Put this on, let the team finish their work, and then go see Tasha."

"I don't know how to thank you."

"Just say thank you. Oh, and make Tasha happy."

"Thank you."

"One last thing. Send me selfies." Maria giggled as she went back to Sophia. She kept Sophia distracted as Megan exited since she wanted this to be a fun surprise for her as well. It was after five thirty when they finished. It had taken a team effort, but they were professionals of the highest caliber and worth every penny. Maria stood up and told Sophia to close her eyes, with no peeking allowed. She personally added the shoes to complete the outfit.

"Sophia. Open your eyes, dear."

"Mommy! You're beautiful! You look like a princess!"

Megan blushed.

"You're right, Sophia. But our princess is missing something."

Maria hurried from the room, returning shortly thereafter. In her hands, she held a silver tiara, which she handed to Sophia. "Here, darling. Put this on your mother." Megan bent down as Sophia placed the tiara in her hair. "Perfect! And now, Princess Megan, your chariot awaits. Technically a limousine, but we'll call it a chariot for now."

CHAPTER 36

PART ONE: IN YOUR EYES

Tasha was feeling much better on Friday after her talk with Megan the night before. Work passed mostly uneventfully. There was a sense of eagerness in the office as the day progressed. The company holiday party typically wasn't a lavish affair, but it had an open bar, and the food was generally really good—although it was hard to get a bad meal in Portland.

Anyway, free food and drinks was fun, plus there was usually a well-stocked raffle. Even Kevin was taking a break from being horrible.

Late afternoon, Tasha was notified that a courier had arrived for her, which was unusual. Opening the package, she found stiletto heels and black stockings, along with a note. *I suspect that you might have forgotten accessories. Love, Maria.* Tasha had been planning on leggings and Doc Martens. She debated whether to stay with her original plan or accept that Maria was meddling and just go along. The leggings and Doc Martens would be comfortable, but the stockings and stilettos did go better with the dress. At quarter after five, Tasha headed for the bathroom to change and make sure that her hair and make-up were in good shape. When she emerged after five thirty, everyone was already on their way to the lounge where the party was being held.

Tasha arrived at the party and said hi to her co-workers. Everyone else was in their work clothes, and Tasha began to feel self-conscious. She made her way to the bar to get a rum and Coke, light on the rum. As she sipped her drink, her anxiety increased. *This was a dumb idea. Why did I invite Megan to this? Why did I wear this stupid dress? Oh yeah—Maria. She's up to something. Well, maybe we can just stay for a few minutes, have a drink, and then go have a girls night like Megan suggested. Oh, great, here comes Kevin.*

"Hi Tasha. When do we meet your plus one?"

"Soon, I hope." *What the hell is that on his head?*

"Are you having a good time?"

"Yeah, how about you?" *Is that a mistletoe hat? At least it's not a belt buckle.*

"I really enjoy these…"

Tasha expected Kevin to go on, but instead he stopped. Actually, everything seemed to stop. The band paused in their setup, the conversations came to a halt, everyone was staring at the door.

Kevin broke the silence, saying, "Who is *that*?"

Tasha turned and followed everyone else's gaze to the door. Framed in the entryway was a woman in an emerald gown, inlaid with silver Celtic triskelion patterns. Her purple, lavender-accented hair was done up in an elegant styling, contrasting with the natural red peeking through at the base. She wore silver gloves and had a silver tiara in her hair. Her green eyes locked on to Tasha's and she smiled.

Tasha answered, her voice barely more than a whisper, "That's my girlfriend."

CHAPTER 36

PART TWO: IN YOUR EYES

Across the silent room, Megan heard Tasha's words. She had been a girlfriend multiple times and then a fiancée and then a wife, but this was different from everything before. This was her best friend, whom she had known for almost half her life. This was the woman that she loved and that loved her back. Tasha had just claimed her in public, and Megan's heart leapt.

Now, it was her turn to publicly lay claim to Tasha, and with that, she stepped forward.

Stiletto heels are generally considered uncomfortable; however, they lend themselves perfectly to a maneuver that Megan had always thought of as The Strut. It was something that you might see in a movie or a stage show. The Strut required balance, grace, and finesse. Most of all, it required perfect confidence. Too much confidence and it became exaggerated and you could break an ankle. Too little confidence and you were probably going to stumble and break an ankle. This was a move in the realm of actresses, drag queens, courtesans, and models.

Megan would never usually try anything like this, but that vast well of anxiety that had been eating at her for days was gone. With her eyes locked onto Tasha's, Megan *strutted*.

Each step brought her closer to her heart's desire. Megan felt her heart thundering against her ribs. The only sounds were the click of her heels and the swish of her dress. The room felt hot and her breath was ragged in her throat. Megan could see the smile forming on Tasha's lips as she watched Megan walk towards her. She felt her own lips curve into an answering smile. Megan felt like a goddess.

Megan felt every eye in the room on her, but only two eyes mattered. Her entire world was there before her, and her smile grew with each step forward.

Reaching Tasha, Megan reached out and touched her arm. "Hello… girlfriend," Megan purred.

"Hello, yourself," Tasha purred back. She pulled Megan into an embrace. Sound returned to the room as everyone shook off their reverie.

"Holy shit," Kevin uttered. "If you need some mistletoe—"

Pulling away from Tasha, Megan's gaze swiveled toward Kevin. "You must be Kevin."

"How did you know?"

"Kevin," she said firmly. "Before I decide to call your company's HR Monday morning and file a complaint about sexual harassment at a company function, why don't you take off that stupid hat and leave us the hell alone."

Kevin blanched and scampered off, pulling off the hat as he went.

The look of surprise and glee on Tasha's face was priceless as she said, "I've wanted to do that for so long. I am so turned on right now."

Megan answered with a playful, yet sultry grin. "By me telling off your boss, or by this dress?"

"Definitely you telling off my boss, but also this dress. Where did you—Maria. She's meddling."

"She is. I feel like I'm okay with it, though. The look on your face…"

"On my face? On everyone's face! Girl, you could have heard a pin drop in here."

"I know! I felt so exposed, and then you called me your girl-friend and I just felt powerful. I really like that, by the way. Girl-friend. That word tastes delicious in my mind."

"Me too! And you called me your girlfriend, didn't you?"

"Yes." Megan blushed crimson as she acknowledged that, but she smiled as well.

"So, girlfriend," Tasha drawled. "Maria got you dolled up for me?"

"Tasha, you should have seen it! Maria hired a professional crew from a TV show. They were amazing!"

"Megan, I think you'd look beautiful in a burlap sack, but wow…"

"Thank you, and you look amazing as well! Oh, we're green and red tonight. Like Christmas!"

"You're so silly, but you're right. Also, where did you learn that walk? I'd break an ankle!"

"The Strut? Watching movies and stuff. I can't believe that I didn't break anything!"

"You were like a goddess! Growing up with my father, he wanted me to read about ancient cultures and their stories. I never understood why so many cultures had goddesses like Ishtar, the Goddess of Love and War, Kali, the midnight-hued Mother and Destroyer, bright-eyed Athena, Goddess of Crafts, Wisdom, and War, whose father so feared her birth that he swallowed her mother whole, or Freya, Goddess of Love, Sex, and War, whose chariot is pulled by two cats."

"Two cats? Really?"

"Yes. As I was saying, I never understood that duality ascribed to so many goddesses until you walked across the room. Like life and death hung in the balance."

"Wow… I mean, in that moment, I felt powerful, but more than anything, I was focused on one thing. The Goddess in front of me."

"Oh, I like it. I guess that we can be goddesses together."

"Right now, though, this particular goddess could use a drink and some food."

"Of course, Megan. Let's get you some food and a drink, and then I'll introduce you to my co-workers."

"As your girlfriend?"

"Definitely!"

The pair made the rounds, chatting with people as they went. Eventually, they found themselves alone at a table where they listened to the band and got caught up on each other's days.

After a bit, Megan said, "I want to dance with my girlfriend." She grabbed Tasha's hand and drew her out onto the dance floor. They danced for a few songs before the band slowed things down. Then they moved close for the slow song, the world falling away as they did. As they swayed to the music, they felt as if there was no one else in the room.

That spell was broken as the band kicked up the tempo. Megan said, "My feet are starting to hurt."

"Me too."

"Tasha…"

"Yeah…"

"Let's get out of here. There's something that I want to do, and I don't want a room full of strangers around."

"What's that?"

"I want to kiss you."

CHAPTER 37
THIS KISS

Tasha felt an electric thrill at Megan's words. She felt her face light up with a smile fueled by that electric feeling. "Where should we go?" she asked.

"I don't know, but we really need to get out of here. Do you need to get a coat?"

"That's my girlfriend, practical as always."

Megan smiled at that.

Tasha continued, "And you really care. That's why you're such an amazing mom."

"Awww, thank you!"

"You're welcome, and no coat. I left it at the office. I'll get it on Monday." Tasha took Megan's hand and they walked toward the door. Once outside, Megan raised an arm and waved. Down the street, headlights turned on and a parked vehicle started to move.

"Maria got us a limo! I haven't ridden in one of these since my wedding."

"Prom for me, and bravo, Maria."

When the limousine pulled up, the two quickly bundled themselves into the warm vehicle. The driver asked where they wanted to go next. Megan answered, "We'd like to go to a nice restaurant.

Something classy but not overdone. I haven't had a chance to look for one, though."

"Leave that to me," he responded before asking, "Any restrictions?"

"No, not that I can think of. You?"

Tasha answered, "No restrictions here. A cozy place with candles would be nice, though."

"Got it! You two just relax and I'll take care of it." With that, the driver raised the divider, leaving them in private.

The two relaxed and shook off their brief foray into the cold evening. They huddled together and took one last selfie for Maria. As Tasha sent the selfie to Maria, she felt Megan's fingers on her biceps, tracing the cat paw trail up her arm.

"Tasha…" Megan purred. "I think that it's time to properly kiss my girlfriend."

"Are you sure? Here in the limo?" Megan's fingertips were leaving trails of fire on her arm.

"Tasha, please kiss me before I lose my nerve."

Tasha leaned in and Megan met her. What started as a brief kiss quickly elongated into a very drawn-out and energetic kiss. Eventually, the two separated and fell backwards, each breathing heavily.

Tasha dreamily asked, "So, how was it?"

"Amazing! Was it good for you? I've never—"

"Shhh, Megan. It was perfect."

"Mmm, good. I think that might have been the best kiss of my life." Megan giggled, then continued, "But I'm not sure. We might have to do that again. You know, for science."

"Well, I guess so." Tasha laughed. "How can I say 'no' to science?"

Tasha was about to sit up when Megan pounced. Suddenly Megan's hands were on her face, in her hair. Megan's lips were on hers, then her tongue invaded Tasha's mouth. Megan straddled her hips, taking advantage of the roominess of the limousine to press Tasha backwards. Tasha wasn't complaining. Not at all, well, at least until she started to have trouble breathing. She tapped out, and Megan sat up, still in Tasha's lap as the limousine lurched into motion. Tasha grabbed her to keep her from falling, and Megan laughed as she held onto Tasha.

"Where did that come from?"

"I don't know, I just felt it at the moment. Was it too much?"

"No, it was incredible. You are incredible."

"Thank you. You are amazing, too!"

"So, Megan. What did science say? Better than the first one?"

"Mmm, definitely. You know, just to make the experiment fair, maybe I should get off your lap and have you pounce on me and kiss me to within an inch of my life? You know, for science."

"I dunno, Megan. I guess I'll have to do it, but only because that makes the experiment fair." Tasha grinned and leapt on top of Megan. She felt Megan's hands on her hips, steadying her as the car rocked and swayed on their way to wherever they were going. Tasha felt like they were crossing a bridge, both literally and figuratively, as Megan's fingers started to trace downwards. They finished crossing the Willamette right about the same time as Megan's fingertips found the tops of her stockings.

With a start, Megan pulled her hands off of Tasha's legs and placed them on her shoulders, gently pushing her back. They were both breathing heavily, and Megan was definitely flushed.

"Tasha, I…"

"What is it, baby?"

"We need to dial this back a bit. I'm sorry."

"Is it too much? I'm sorry, I didn't—"

"Tasha, you are good! Better than good, actually." Megan leered at her. "I really love kissing you, and I want to do a lot more of that, but that's as far as we can go right now."

"Oh?"

"Yeah, I'm sorry. I'm still married to Brad and I swore a vow to be faithful. Sure, he's a cheating shitweasel—" Tasha grinned at that "—but I am not."

"No, you're definitely not a cheating shitweasel."

"Thank you, Tasha. I'm sorry if I'm disappointing you."

"Megan, it's okay. We both need to be comfortable. I'm gonna tell you, Brad better sign those damn papers soon or else I'm gonna rip his arms off and beat him to death with them!" Megan laughed at that. Tasha continued, "Even then, let's promise to talk and be sure that we are comfortable. If we go beyond where either of us is comfortable, let's promise to communicate that and be okay with it."

"Oh, Goddess Tasha. You make consent sound so sexy!" They both laughed at that. "But yes, you are right and I promise to communicate with you."

"Me too. Any idea where we're going?"

"We definitely crossed a bridge."

"Yeah, we did," Tasha agreed with an over-the-top lasciviousness.

Megan answered in a very sultry tone, "So. Stockings?"

"Do you like them?"

"Definitely," Megan's voice dropped to a silky murmur. "You should wear them again some time."

"What should I wear them with?"

"Who said that you would be wearing anything else?"

Tasha felt her spine tingle at that.

"Oh look, we've stopped!"

"I'm gonna get you back for that, Megan!"

"Mmm, I'm looking forward to it."

Before Tasha could respond, the driver tapped on the divider. They quickly readjusted themselves and rolled down the divider. "We're here," he said. "I hope that this place works for you."

"This Thai place? It looks perfect, thank you!"

"Parking is terrible around here. This is my card. Call me when you're ready."

"Thanks! Are you hungry? We can get you some take-out."

"You ladies are really sweet. I always pack something. If you're gonna be here for a while, I may hit a food cart for something hot."

Tasha looked at Megan, then said, "Yes, I think that we'll probably be here for an hour or so."

They exchanged pleasantries as Megan and Tasha exited the car. They held hands as they walked into the restaurant, partially because they really enjoyed that and partially because they were both wearing stilettos and needed the help balancing. The driver had arranged a table for them, so they were seated immediately. The restaurant had a decent crowd, but not overwhelming. Once they ordered, they held hands across the table.

Tasha broke the silence between them. "I don't want to pressure you, but, um, now that we are officially girlfriends—" they both smiled at that "—are you still thinking of moving out at some point, or do you want to make this permanent?"

"About that. I really want to stay with you, and I like your apartment and all, but... oh, wow. I know I'm blushing now. Tasha, I think that Sophia needs her own bedroom!"

Tasha's eyebrows arched. "Megan, are you saying that you want to sleep with me?"

"Yes! Very much, yes. I mean, right now I want to sleep with you, at least until the divorce is finalized, and then I want to *sleep with you* and I definitely can't do that with Sophia there."

Tasha relished the emphasis that Megan added and the quiet urgency in her voice. "Agreed. When do you want to start looking for a new place?"

"Right now! I mean, not right now, right now, but you know…"

"Let's start looking, then. I like my apartment, but I'm really motivated now to get Sophia her own room. We might need sound-proofing."

"Tasha!"

"Just saying." Tasha couldn't help the feral grin on her face.

Their dumplings arrived right then, saving a wildly blushing Megan from more embarrassment. Dinner came along not long after that. They called the driver once they were finished and held hands again on their way to the limousine, which would take them back to Maria's place.

Tasha kept holding Megan's hand, even once inside. "I'm really having fun tonight, and not just the wildly passionate make-out session."

"Me too. We should get dressed up and go out on date nights more often."

"That's a good thought! I'm really enjoying jumping into this relationship with you, but I think that it would be good for us to go on dates. I feel like it's really different for us because we lived together for four years and then have known each other for ten more years."

And the rest of our lives sounds really good right now. Hopefully Megan thinks that as well.

"That makes sense to me. I've never had a girlfriend before and I'm really excited to go out with you. Oh, I get to show the world how beautiful and sexy my girlfriend is." By the tone in her voice, it seemed like Megan was as giddy as Tasha felt.

"I bet that your girlfriend is just as beautiful and sexy as my girlfriend is."

"I bet she is! Oh, but does your girlfriend kiss you as well as me?"

"Mmm, let's find out."

"For sci—mmpf."

CHAPTER 38

TAKE ME HOME TONIGHT/BE MY BABY

Megan and Tasha apologized to the driver for not having cash for a tip, but he assured them that Maria tended to be very generous. They got out and walked hand-in-hand to Maria's door, which promptly opened to allow them entrance. Maria saw their entwined hands and asked, "So, how was your evening?"

Tasha answered, "It was very good."

Maria grinned at that. "Oh, really?"

"Stop prying, Maria. And thank you for meddling."

"Of course, dear! I do enjoy spoiling my friends, especially when they need it."

Megan jumped into the conversation, "How is Sophia? Did she behave alright?"

"She was an angel! She's sleeping now, in case the two of you wish to extend your evening…"

"Thank you, Maria. That's very kind, but I think we'll be heading home now. Where is she?"

"She fell asleep on the couch over here. She dearly wanted to stay awake until you returned, but she couldn't keep her eyes open."

"Aw! Tasha, can you get her coat and things? I'll get her up.

You might have to drive."

"Sure thing!"

"In the hall closet, dear." Tasha walked away and Megan had to drag her eyes away from her girlfriend's retreating form. Maria continued, "Now that she's gone, how are you feeling, Megan?"

"I'm very happy. Thank you again, Maria. For watching Sophia and for all of this." She gestured to her attire. "Oh, when should I return this?"

"You're very welcome, and please, it's yours. That dress is perfect for you."

"I—"

"Spoiling my friends, dear. Enjoy!"

"Thank you." Megan bent down to gently rouse Sophia. "Wake up, sweetheart. It's time to go home now."

"Hi, Mommy," Sophia said sleepily.

"Make sure that you thank Ms. Rodriguez for watching you this evening."

"Thank you, Ms. Rodriguez."

"You are quite welcome, Sophia. You are welcome any time." Maria looked at Megan. "I mean that."

"That's very kind of you. We may take you up on that. Okay, let's get you home, sweetie."

"There's our sleepy angel!"

"Aunt Tasha! You look so pretty!"

Tasha is gorgeous. I always knew that she was pretty, but now I'm starting to feel *just how pretty she is.*

"Thank you, angel."

"Aunt Tasha, doesn't Mommy look like a princess?"

"She does. The most beautiful princess ever."

Megan smiled at her over Sophia's head. *I'm your princess, and you are mine, Tasha. I feel like Sleeping Beauty, except I was woken up by the kiss of a beautiful princess.*

They said their goodbyes to Maria and bundled Sophia into Megan's Subaru. Once home, Megan put Sophia to bed while

Tasha fed a very excited Nocturne. They both collapsed on the couch and helped each other remove their stilettos.

"Oh, that feels good."

"Yes. I like the look, and holy shit, you were hot in those, but I'm so glad to take them off."

"Me too."

"Wow… what a night."

"Yeah, it was. Tasha?"

"Hmm?"

"I'm really tired, but before tonight ends, I want one more dance with you."

"That sounds perfect. Which song?"

"You pick. Something slow and sweet."

"I know just the song." Tasha quickly tapped into her phone as they stood up. They embraced and slowly swayed to Peter Gabriel's "In Your Eyes." Megan murmured, "Perfect."

"Are you crying?"

"Happy tears. I've never been so happy before. I love you, Tasha."

"I love you too, and I love our family."

CHAPTER 39

I KISSED A GIRL

Megan was up early on Saturday morning. She got the coffee started, grabbed her laptop and plopped down on the couch. Her first order of business was to search for a two-bedroom apartment. This task became significantly more difficult when Nocturne walked in and decided that Megan's lap was exactly where she wanted to be. It took some maneuvering, but Nocturne eventually settled herself in the nook created by Megan's legs, while Megan balanced the laptop precariously on one knee, her searching occasionally interrupted by a head bonk. The cat was happy, which was what was truly important.

Megan identified some opportunities, which she flagged for review with Tasha. One was a unit in their building, which would be incredibly convenient.

After a while, Megan's need for coffee and breakfast achieved a higher priority than her desire to ensure that Nocturne had a comfortable leg nook to rest in. Nocturne strongly disagreed and stalked off in a huff, her tail twitching furiously as she went in search of another human to snuggle.

As she poured herself some coffee, Megan could hear vague cat-related noises coming from Tasha. She poured a second mug after seeing Tasha flit from the bedroom to the bathroom. Tasha stumbled sleepily into the living room as Megan silently admired her disheveled beauty. She held out a mug and was rewarded with a grateful smile. She waited until Tasha had taken a sip, then leaned in for a kiss, which was granted.

"Good morning!"

"Ugh, how are you so cheerful? How long have you been up?"

"About an hour or so."

"Your hair is a mess."

"I know. There's enough hairspray in there to hold up a building. I'll take a shower soon."

"Mmm, can I help?"

"Oh, that's tempting, but I'll have to defer that to when we have a private bathroom."

"Sorry, I should have thought of that. My horniness carried me away."

"It's no problem, and I like how you think. How did you sleep?"

"I slept amazing until a little toe assassin attacked my feet."

"Ah, that's what I heard. Sorry about that. She was resting with me and then left when I got up. She must have taken out her anger on your poor toes."

"Mmm hmm, so it's your fault. Well, she was snuggling up to Sophia as I left."

The pair returned to sipping their coffee, enjoying being in each other's company. Megan broke the silence and said in a sing-song voice, "Ta-sha… Guess what?"

"What?"

"I have a giiiiiiirlfriiiiiiiieeeeend."

"Why are you so annoyingly cute?"

"It's a super power."

"Ugh. If I kiss you again, will you be less annoying?"

Megan grinned impishly. "Maybe. Mmpf."

"That's better."

If I had known kissing Tasha felt this good back in college, I— I better not go down that road. We are here now and that makes me happy.

Megan laughed and Tasha laughed with her. "So, I started looking for a new apartment. I've found a few places in this area. Want to take a look?"

"Sure! Just in this area, or have you been looking at other parts of the city?"

"I focused on this area since you already have a regular commute and I really don't want to put Sophia in a third school this year."

"That makes sense. Look, this one is just down the hall."

"Yeah, I thought that might be convenient."

"Let's look at the other options and see if we like anything better than this." They spent some time browsing the various options that Megan had identified and eventually decided to see if the unit down the hall was still available.

"Great, let me go and wash all this hairspray out of my hair and then we can go down to the office." About the time that Megan finished, Sophia was waking up, so the trip to the office was delayed by the flurry of activity as Sophia and Nocturne were fed. Tasha went to grab a quick shower and Megan cleaned up in the kitchen, smiling to herself and humming.

Once they were both ready, they went down to the office. Tasha introduced Megan as her girlfriend and inquired about the availability of the two-bedroom apartment. The office manager gave them a tour of the unit and they agreed to take it. After that, they went and signed the paperwork. The office manager was a bit surprised that they wanted the keys today, but she didn't object.

"This is crazy. You know that, right?"

Megan looked at Tasha in alarm. "Is this too fast? Should we go back and tell her to rip up the lease?"

"No… Maybe… I mean… I want this so much and I love the idea of having our own place with more space. It's just, this is so brand new and now I'm freaking out."

Megan reached out to hold Tasha. "I thought that it was my job to freak out about moving too fast." She smiled and continued, "I'll admit that I'm scared, too. We've lived together before, but this is very different. This is incredibly risky and we probably should have talked more, but I'm so excited to be taking this leap with you."

"You are? I'm excited, too, even though I'm anxious. I feel like we would have gotten to this decision eventually. We just, you know, skipped ahead a couple of weeks."

"We really did, but I know that everything will work out amazingly. I appreciate how you welcomed us into your home, and now we're going to have our own place." Megan hugged her close.

"I have no idea how you are so calm right now."

"Can I tell you how much I love being the one telling you that everything's going to be okay?"

"You're enjoying this, aren't you?"

"Honestly, I'm mostly enjoying holding you."

"You've discovered my secret." Tasha pulled back and smiled at her. "Now, let's get back home. We have a *lot* of work ahead of us."

By the time they reached their door it seemed like Tasha had dialed back from the brink of panic. Megan's enthusiasm seemed to be rubbing off on her, and they were holding hands and giggling as they walked through the door.

"Hi, sweetie! We're back."

"Hi Mommy!"

"Come on, Sophia. I want to show you our new home."

"Are we not going to live with Aunt Tasha anymore?" Sophia didn't look happy.

"Oh, no. Aunt Tasha is moving with us. We're moving to a new place so that you can have your own room."

As crazy as committing to living together is, it feels even more crazy not to do this. I really hope that Tasha agrees.

"Will you have your own room too, Mommy?"

"Um…"

Tasha leaned in and whispered, "This is all you."

Sophia asked, "Mommy, will you and Aunt Tasha sleep in the other room?"

"Mhm. Sleep, among other things," Tasha whispered with a sultry tone.

"Yes, sweetie."

"Why can't I sleep with you like I do now?"

"Because you'll have your own bedroom!"

"…and because your Mommy has certain needs," Tasha breathed huskily in her ear.

"Stop it! You're so bad!" Megan hissed. They both giggled while Sophia looked on with confusion. Megan reached out to grab her daughter's hand. Tasha led them down the hall, holding Megan's other hand. When they got to their new apartment, Megan asked, "Do you have your keys? My hands are a bit full." Tasha's head turned and she saw the mischievous grin on her face. "Tasha, don't even say it!"

"What? You don't know what I was going to say."

"Oh, I think I know."

Tasha pouted as she opened the door. Megan showed Sophia around the empty apartment and then let her loose in what would soon be her bedroom. As she walked back to Tasha, she said, "You have a dirty mind."

"Takes one to know—mmpf!" Megan shut her up with a kiss. "Mmmm, our first kiss in our new home."

"First of many."

I never thought that kissing another woman would feel this good. Maybe it wouldn't be the same if it were anyone besides Tasha. I'll probably never know, and I am perfectly fine with that.

"Okay, Mom, I like my new room."

"That's great, angel. We need to get you a bed now."

"Yes, now!" Tasha whispered.

I completely agree.

They all walked back to their soon-to-be former home. Megan was doing her best to answer Sophia's questions, while Tasha was doing her best to distract her with whispered double entendres. She was furiously shushing Tasha when Sophia asked, "Mommy, why are you being so weird?"

"What?" *Well, that question shut Tasha up.*

"You and Aunt Tasha keep whispering and giggling. It's not fair if you don't tell me!"

"Um, Aunt Tasha keeps whispering grown-up jokes, which she really shouldn't do because it is so unfair to you." Megan pointedly added a meaningful glare directed at Tasha.

"You also kissed Aunt Tasha."

Uh oh…

"I did. Are you okay with that?"

"It's yucky!"

Uh oh! "Sophia, is it yucky because I kissed another girl or is it yucky because kissing is yucky?"

"Kissing is yucky!"

Yes! "So, you don't mind that your mom kissed Aunt Tasha?"

"I like Aunt Tasha!"

"But kissing is yucky? Because I'm about to kiss you to pieces!" Megan started feverishly kissing her daughter, who squealed with laughter.

"Aunt Tasha, make her stop!"

"Are you sure, munchkin?"

"Yes! Save me, Aunt Tasha."

Megan felt a hand on your shoulder and heard Tasha say, "Come here, you! Time for a taste of your own medicine." Suddenly, Megan was attacked by kisses, much in the same manner as what she had just done to her daughter. Soon, Megan was the one squealing with laughter.

Tasha finally relented, leaving Megan panting desperately between residual laughs. She watched as Tasha sat back on the couch and said to Sophia, "Munchkin, I know that kisses are yucky, but maybe you'd be willing to kiss your Aunt Tasha on the cheek to thank her for saving you?"

Sophia planted a kiss on Tasha's cheek and then hugged her fiercely. "I love you, Aunt Tasha."

She's really good with Sophia. I'm so glad that Sophia likes her, too.

Megan hugged the two of them. "I love you both."

CHAPTER 40
CONFIDENT

It wasn't even noon, and they had a long day ahead of them. Tasha was already deep into a mental prioritization list, a habit which was helping her stave off the lingering panic surrounding their snap decision to move into a whole new apartment. The first order of business was to get Sophia set up for her new room, which was definitely a "Megan task." It was too early for lunch, but getting further from breakfast, so Tasha tucked a granola bar into Megan and Sophia's coats as she directed them off to Ikea. That should give her two or three hours to work alone. The top priority in any move was always the bed, because no matter what the state of everything else was, you needed a place to sleep. Because they were staying in the same building, Tasha put that in the "flex" category. She decided that they would move the bed only after Sophia's new room was set.

That left her moving further down her list to find items that she could handle alone. Clothes and the kitchen fit that description. Tasha started in the closet, quickly sorting items into three piles: Definitely Yes; Let's See If Megan Wants It; and This Needs To Go. Once done, she moved the Definitely Yes pile and got that hung up in the new place. A quick run to the store netted some boxes, then she started on moving the kitchen. As the kitchens were nearly identical, that was fairly simple, albeit tiring. Tasha was over half done with the kitchen when Sophia found her.

"Mommy needs help with some big boxes, Aunt Tasha."

"Alright, let me grab a jacket." Sophia practically dragged her out to Megan's packed Subaru.

"Is there anything left in the store?"

"Haha. You're so funny," Megan responded sarcastically. "I think that we're going to need to move some smaller items before we get to the big boxes."

"Yeah, looks like it."

It took multiple trips, accompanied by numerous unflattering comments directed in the general direction of Sweden, but they got the car unloaded. Panting, they surveyed the scattered boxes of many sizes in the new apartment. "Pizza?" Tasha asked.

"Yes!"

"Okay, let me order some. What would you like?" Tasha placed the order, trying not to be distracted by watching Megan working the kinks out of her back. "Done! This is so much harder than when we were in college."

"Duh! In college, we could just bat our eyelashes at some frat boys and things would get moved."

"I wonder if that would still work?"

"I feel like it would. You're hotter than you were in college, and I'm doing alright."

"More than alright," Tasha purred.

Ten years after college and being a mom and Megan is somehow more beautiful than ever. Damn, I am lucky.

"Down, girl! There's one critical flaw in your idea, though."

"What's that?"

"The complete lack of frat boys to bat our eyelashes at."

"That *is* a problem. Maybe we should knock on some doors and see if there are any lonely men?"

"Tasha, we are strong, independent women. We got this," Megan added with mock sternness.

"Yes, we are, but my back isn't feeling that feminist spirit right now."

"Tell your back that I'll rub it later."

Tasha grinned lasciviously. "Suddenly, I feel much better."

Megan responded breezily, "Great! Let's get Sophia's bed set up then!"

Tasha could only groan in response. The pizza blessedly arrived somewhere around page eight of the pictographic instructions. After they devoured half of the pizza, it was back to work. Sophia was in charge of handing them supplies while the two adults put things together. Once they got the hang of the instructions, things moved quickly. Megan kept most of the clothes, since most of her stuff was still at Brad's (a problem for another day). Moving their bed and the couch was a more arduous process, accompanied by much swearing. Sophia moved all of Nocturne's items while they were doing this. The final act of moving, at least for Saturday, was when Tasha carried Nocturne to their new home. Nocturne quickly explored the new space, tail standing high with the tip twitching.

After that, it was time to relax and finish the remainder of the pizza. Tasha was very thankful when Megan handed her a hard cider. She felt like they had definitely earned that. Tasha joined Megan on the couch after dinner, both of them wearily watching Sophia using a string toy to play with Nocturne. It was a peaceful domestic scene, right until Sophia declared, "We need a brother or sister."

Tasha felt Megan stiffen beside her as her own panic level started to rise. "What was that, sweetheart?" Megan asked.

"I think that Nocturne might like a brother or sister."

Tasha relaxed, although she felt Megan's wariness next to her. "Let me talk about that with your Aunt Tasha, okay? Um, Sophia. Is this your way of saying that you would also like a brother or sister?"

With that, Tasha's panic came roaring back.

"No, Mommy. I'm okay. I just want Nocturne to have a friend while I'm at school."

With that, they both relaxed. Tasha added, "That's very sweet, munchkin. I promise that I will talk about it with your mom."

"Thanks! Aunt Tasha?"

"Yes?"

"Are you going to be my new mommy?"

Tasha was stunned by the question. She wasn't sure how to answer that, a situation not helped when Megan leaned in and whispered, "This is all you." She could practically hear the smile in Megan's voice.

Damn it, Megan. Okay, breathe. This is only the most important oral exam of your life, courtesy of an eight-year-old.

"Um… Well, you will always have your mom. That will never change. But I would love to be your second mom, if you're okay with that."

"I'd like that!"

"I mean, if it's okay with your mom."

"Is it okay, Mommy?"

"Yes, that's wonderful, sweetheart."

"I'm gonna call you Mama Tasha now."

Wow, I aced that test. And I love that title more than I ever would have thought possible.

Tasha's heart was thrilled at that. "I love it!" She gave Sophia a big hug. Then, she grinned evilly and stage whispered, "Now, munchkin, I need your help convincing your mom to make it official."

Megan glared at her over Sophia's head, but Tasha could tell that her glare didn't have much force behind it.

Everyone was getting tired by that point, so they put Sophia to bed in her own room not long after. Once that was done, Tasha and Megan got ready for bed in their own private bathroom. Tasha flopped down on the bed and mumbled, "I seem to remember something about a back rub."

"Of course, my love."

She felt Megan start to work on the kinks in her back. It felt amazing, but then Megan stopped. Tasha grunted in protest, and then felt her shirt rising as Megan slipped her hands underneath. Megan went back to work, kneading at Tasha's sore muscles. *Mmmm, the first way was good, but this... this is amazing for real.* Once again, Megan stopped and Tasha grunted in protest.

"This won't do," Tasha heard Megan whisper. "Lift up." Tasha continued to grunt in protest, but lifted herself onto her elbows. That's when she felt Megan grab hold of the hem of her shirt and slide it over her head. Megan gently pushed her back down onto the bed and maneuvered the shirt completely off. Megan went back to work on her back. *This is MUCH better,* Tasha thought as she drifted off to sleep.

CHAPTER 41

I WOULD DO ANYTHING FOR LOVE (BUT I WON'T DO THAT)

Tasha slowly surfaced from a deep, relaxed sleep. Yesterday had been long and tiring, but very productive. She felt confident that they could finish the move today. But right now it just felt good to stay cocooned in these sheets… Sheets that were touching the bare skin of her chest! Relief flooded in when she remembered that Sophia was sleeping in her own room.

What happened last night? We put Sophia to bed. Then we got into bed. I think our clothes were on. Then Megan started giving me a back rub. Then my shirt came off. I can't remember much after that. Ummm… Tasha reached down to check. *I still have panties on, so we probably didn't do anything too crazy.*

She could hear Megan gently snoring next to her. *Well, it's definitely been a very long time since I woke up like this with another person in my bed.* Tasha rolled over and studied the back of Megan's head. She could see Megan's natural red hair, intermingled with a few grays, peeking out from underneath the waves of purple.

Mmm, I'm good with this. Damn, she looks good. Of course, the moment she thought that, Megan farted in her sleep. *Yep, still good with this.*

Tasha lay there for a few minutes, just enjoying the peaceful morning. Eventually, though, she got curious. Tasha shuffled closer to Megan and reached over, gently touching Megan's shoulder blades. Feeling no shirt there, her fingertips traced downwards.

Okay, panties are there. Did I take off her shirt? Did she? She has a really nice ass.

Megan grunted and Tasha quickly pulled her hand away. *Please say she didn't feel me grabbing her ass.*

"Tasha," Megan mumbled, "were you just feeling my ass?"

"Um. I was just checking to see if you were still wearing anything."

"Uh huh…"

I hope that she's okay with that. "And, um, you are, so that's good."

"Uh huh…"

Is it a bad sign that she hasn't turned over? Does she sound amused? I should probably stop talking. Why can't I stop talking?

"I woke up without my shirt and then I made sure that I still had panties on."

"Uh huh…"

She definitely sounds amused now.

"And then I found out that you didn't have a shirt on, and um…"

"Uh huh…"

Did she just giggle?

"I couldn't remember anything after you took my shirt off and rubbed my back, and I wanted to make sure that we didn't… you know… do stuff."

"So, you were feeling my ass while I was asleep because you were worried that I took advantage of you in your sleep?"

She's not really angry, right? Because I'm not sure.

"Um, when you put it like that, it sounds really bad."

"Uh huh…"

I'm pretty sure that she's smiling. She needs to roll over because I can't tell. Why can't I stop talking?

"I didn't mean… um, I'm sorry that I was feeling your ass."

"So, you didn't like feeling my ass?"

"No! Your ass is amazing! I, uh—"

"Are you really sorry about feeling my ass, then?"

She's definitely teasing me now. Oh, Goddess, I really want to feel her ass again, too.

"Kinda? I mean, I guess that I'm sorry about not asking you if I could feel your incredible ass first. I definitely should have asked first, but you were asleep, and I was worried that…"

"Tasha?"

"Yeah?"

"Would you like to feel my ass again?"

"…yes?"

"You have my permission to feel my ass."

Yes!

"Oh, goody! Um, Megan? Why aren't you wearing a shirt?"

Definitely the best butt that I have ever laid my hands on.

"Well, you fell asleep while I was rubbing your back, so I couldn't put your shirt back on. And then it felt weird that I had a shirt on and you didn't and even though you were asleep, I just thought it was only fair that I sleep like this."

"Did you like it?"

Megan paused. "Yeah, I did. Um, Tasha? Hands outside of my underwear."

"Sorry, I got carried away."

"I'm glad that my ass is that enticing. Tasha?"

"Yeah?"

"Can I snuggle back against you?"

"Um, sure."

"Mmmm, that feels… different. But really good. I'm sorry about teasing you."

"No, you're not."

Tasha heard Megan's giggle, but she also felt it as Megan's back shuddered against her nipples, sending a whole new wave of sensations through Tasha's body.

There was an unmistakable tone of mischief in Megan's voice when she answered, "No, I'm not really sorry."

"You know that we can't stay like this all day, right?"

Tasha felt Megan reach back and take her hand and place it onto her stomach. "I know that we can't. But I just want you to hold me like this for a few minutes, okay?"

A few minutes. Forever. Whatever you want. Please tell me you want that, too.

"I can do that. Megan?"

"Yes?"

"This is us now, right?"

"What do you mean?"

"We took this huge, crazy step and we're not going back? I'm not the rebound girl, right?"

"No, we're not going back. I mean, I guess technically you're the rebound girl, but you're not a rebound. Are you okay?"

"Sorry, I'm having a bit of an anxiety attack. I'm just incredibly happy and I haven't felt like this since I can't remember when and now I'm terrified that you'll leave me and it's stupid and…"

Megan rolled over to face her. "Tasha, it's normal to be anxious. Trust me, of all people, I get that. I have similar worries and I'm still working to wrap my head around the idea of being in love with another woman, but that's the thing. I love you and I'm not going anywhere. Sophia loves you, too, 'Mama Tasha.' So, yeah… We aren't going anywhere."

Tasha felt her anxiety subside and she gently kissed Megan. "I love you, too, Megan."

CHAPTER 42

YOU ARE THE FIRST, THE LAST, MY EVERYTHING

Megan and Tasha started quietly moving the rest of the stuff from the old apartment while Sophia slept in. Once she was up, they decided to take a break. Megan asked Tasha if she would mind making Sophia breakfast while she went out to get them coffee and hot chocolate. Tasha relished the opportunity to be Mama Tasha for a bit and agreed.

After breakfast, they spent a couple more hours finishing the move and cleaning up the old place to avoid any penalties. While they were cleaning, they discussed the pros and cons of getting a second cat. It wasn't a long discussion as both were generally in favor of the idea.

They did a final check to be sure that everything was moved, said a wistful goodbye to their first home together, and then returned the keys.

Back in their new home, Megan suggested, "Tasha, go clean up while I fix lunch for us." She watched Tasha walk away and noted the suggestive wink that she gave her before she disappeared into the bedroom.

"Sophia, would you like to help me make grilled cheese sandwiches for lunch?"

"I'm resting, Mommy."

"I would really like it if you helped me, okay?"

"Yes, Mom…"

"Here's a knife, bread, and butter. Please butter all of the bread while I get the tomato soup going." Once the soup was going, Megan grabbed the step stool for Sophia and delegated the soup stirring to her while she cooked the grilled cheese. "Sophia, I'm sorry that we didn't have much time to talk earlier. Did you like sleeping in your new room?"

"I liked it! Nocturne slept by my feet most of the night."

"That's sweet. I'm glad that she kept you company. Were you okay without me sleeping in the same bed with you?"

"Yeah, you poked me in your sleep sometimes and you snore. So I was okay sleeping by myself. Were you okay sleeping with Mama Tasha?"

Megan blushed a bit at that. "Um, yes. We were okay. I mean, I liked sleeping with your Aunt… Mama Tasha. Oh, I hope that I didn't poke her in the night." *I'm so glad that Tasha didn't hear me say that.* "And since everyone keeps accusing me of snoring, even though I don't snore, I hope that I didn't keep her up."

"Mommy, you *do* snore."

"Didn't you say that Mommy is a princess? Well, princesses don't snore."

Sophia pondered this for a moment, then said, "Princesses definitely snore! That's how Prince Charming was able to find Sleeping Beauty."

Mmmm, in my case, Princess Charming.

Megan definitely didn't remember that part of the story, but the reasoning was pretty good. "Fine, maybe I do snore, but I don't snore much. Like little cat snores."

"Nope! Bear snores."

"Ugh, and I can't even tickle you for that because you are stirring the soup." Sophia grinned triumphantly.

Once Tasha finished showering, they all ate lunch. After they finished, Megan said, "Alright, I'm going to wash off this morning's dirt and dust, and then we can all go to the cat shelter. Maybe we can find a friend for Nocturne."

Sophia was elated. "Mommy, can I choose Nocturne's friend?"

Megan laughed. "Of course, although I think that it is more likely that a cat will choose us."

Tasha added, "That's usually how it works."

Sophia and Tasha had met all of those cats while Megan had only interacted with a few when they were there weeks ago.

It's amazing just how much my life has changed in such a short time.

After meeting and interacting with a few cats, they all agreed on adopting Julius, the big creamsicle floof that had napped in Megan's lap. Once the paperwork was filled out and they took Julius home, they all tried to think of a new name. Not finding a name that they liked better, they stuck with Julius. He would live in Megan and Tasha's bathroom for a few days, at least until Nocturne got used to him.

For her part, Nocturne was already adjusting to a new space, so she took the presence of a new feline to be just another one of the many indignities that she must suffer as part of this new living space. Which is all to say that Julius was just another thing for Nocturne to be curious about.

Tasha needed some time to work on freelance projects, so Megan and Sophia spent some time reading together on the couch. Megan really wanted to help Sophia organize her room, but she sensed that her daughter needed a break from all of the moving-related activities. So long as Sophia had what she needed for school tomorrow, everything else could wait a bit.

Plus, reading together was really enjoyable. She savored that quiet bond between them.

Megan looked up from her book and surveyed their little family. Sophia on the other end of the couch, reading voraciously. A sleeping Nocturne in the middle, draped across their feet. Tasha tapped away at her laptop at the table nearby.

I gave up almost everything I ever knew and somehow ended up with everything I ever wanted.

Tasha looked up at her briefly, smiled, and then returned to her work. Megan answered Tasha's smile with one of her own, and then went back to reading.

The rest of the evening passed much like that. They ate a simple but tasty dinner of linguine in a pesto sauce. Afterwards, they each did their own thing, but comfortably together until it was Sophia's bedtime. Megan helped her get changed and brush her teeth and then Tasha read her a bedtime story.

Once Megan came out of their bathroom she found Tasha sitting on their bed, wearing a nightshirt and scrolling through her phone. Tasha looked up and smiled warmly at her. As she pulled back the covers, Megan thought back to that morning and how they had woken up.

Megan had set her limits on certain aspects of her relationship with Tasha, but that left a lot of gray areas, both in their relationship and in the space between where Megan had always assumed her sexuality was defined and the reality that she was in love with another woman and what that meant. She felt the desire to explore those gray areas, at least a little. Megan reached down to grab the hem of her nightshirt.

Except for my doctor, I haven't taken my shirt off in front of another woman since college softball. Can I do this?

She saw Tasha's eyes follow her hands down and then they followed her hands up as she lifted her shirt. Megan saw Tasha's eyes widen before her shirt covered her eyes. Given Tasha's lurid flirting of late, Megan was surprised that Tasha was looking her in the eyes rather than further south. Feeling exposed, Megan hurried under the covers. She still watched though as Tasha stood up and languidly removed her own nightshirt before slipping into bed.

Holy shit, that was hot. She was definitely putting a little extra into that.

They lay there looking at each other before Tasha spoke, "Thank you, Megan. I suspect that you were pushing the boundaries of your comfort zone." Tasha reached her hand out above the blankets.

Megan took Tasha's hand and squeezed. "I, uh… Thank you for being patient with me. I've always thought of myself one way and it's scary for me to think about myself differently. But in some ways, it's easy, too. I love you, and I know that you love me and are there for me."

"I do love you, Megan, and of course I will be patient with you."

"Thank you. I guess what I'm trying to say is that I'm discovering that what's more important than whether I think of myself as straight or gay or anything is that you are the person that I love and want to spend my life with. I mean, it is important, because so many people have fought so long for equality and it seems like those rights could be stripped away in a heartbeat by a bunch of assholes. There's a lot going on in my head right now."

"I totally get that. I think you asked me before if I was a lesbian, or bisexual, or pansexual, and I didn't have an answer because I'm still figuring myself out. I still don't have that answer, and that's okay. I've got a couple years headstart on you, so don't feel like you need to have the answer now. I do know that I am very much a Megansexual and that feels amazing. Let's continue to talk, to check in with each other, and do what we are both okay with. So long as we do that, everything will work itself out."

"I needed that, Tasha. I just am getting in my own way."

"And you still took a step tonight. You are stronger than you know."

"I did, didn't I?"

"You did and I'm very proud of you. Now, can I see them again?"

CHAPTER 43

DREAM ON

Tasha grumpily turned off her alarm on Monday, rolled over, and closed her eyes. "I hate Monday."

"Me too. I'm really tired after this weekend, but really happy, too."

Tasha felt Megan's hand grasp hers. Tasha opened her eyes and looked over to see Megan smiling at her.

It's honestly not fair that anyone is that gorgeous when they just woke up.

"I wasn't expecting such a crazy weekend, but I am so glad that it happened. Thank you for talking in bed last night. I felt like we were back in college and it made me realize all over again just how much you mean to me."

"Thank you, I really enjoyed that, too. Although, in college we were in different beds and we weren't topless. I think that this is a big improvement."

"Oh, definitely. Megan, last night as we were talking… Something about being skin to skin while we talked about our future and our hopes and dreams… I guess that I really felt our love on a deeper level."

"I really felt that, too. It was like we were just melting together. Your skin is amazing, by the way."

"Yours, too." Tasha couldn't help but smirk when she added, "And, your boobs are absolutely fantastic."

"Fantastic boobs, really? By the way, Tasha, have I ever told you that you look stunning, even with bedhead?"

"Um, no. But thank you! I was just thinking how unfair it was that anyone was as gorgeous as you are when you just woke up."

"Thank you, too. We should probably stop admiring each other and actually get up."

"You are no fun at all."

"Take that back! I'm fun! Hey, speaking of fun, what do you think about setting our alarms earlier and getting in some yoga to start our day?"

Tasha groaned. "You want to get up *earlier*? What kind of monster are you?"

"Trust me. It gets the blood flowing and really helps your energy levels throughout the day. I used to do that most mornings, you know, before we came to live with you. I kinda miss that routine."

How is Megan so enthusiastic about this?

"I'm not sure about this, but we can try it tomorrow."

"Yay! See, now we're both pushing our comfort zones. Okay, let me go see if Sophia is awake."

"Uh, Megan? You might want to put a shirt on first."

"Oh my gosh! Good call!"

She's super pretty when she blushes like that, too.

They set about their morning routine, which was slightly different with a new place, but not much. The biggest challenge was keeping Julius in their bathroom and keeping Nocturne out. Both cats were very curious about each other. As usual, Megan was out the door first.

Today she was headed to a middle school for the first time. Tasha walked Sophia to school. She really enjoyed this part of her new morning routine. It probably wouldn't last much longer. All too soon, Sophia would be in middle school and probably wouldn't want Tasha walking her to school every day. That realization was bittersweet as it also revealed how much Tasha was looking forward to being part of Sophia's life as she grew up.

They let go of each other's hands when they reached the school. Tasha bent down and said, "Sophia, I love you, and I hope that you have a great day."

"I love you, too, Mama Tasha!" She gave Tasha a big hug before running off to join a gaggle of new friends.

Smiling, Tasha headed for the bus stop. On her commute, she checked her phone and saw an email from Brad.

It read:

Hey Tasha,

I finished both of the books that you asked me to read. I haven't written a book report in twenty years and I don't know how to start. It's important to say that reading these books really opened my eyes to the horrible injustices inflicted on Black Americans. Not just Black Americans. The system has been weighted to favor guys like me from the start and that impacts everyone. I'm very sorry for the hurt that I caused you with my ignorance. I'm sorry for hurting Megan and Sophia. I'm sorry for being a pile of shit, as you said. I'm going to do better. I'm going to be better. As you said, so that Sophia can be proud of me, but also so that I can be proud of me.

Regards,
Brad

Tasha emailed back:

Brad,

Not the greatest book report of all time, but I'll spare you the bad envelope. Life is a journey, not a destination and you've hopefully started down a new road on that journey. Now go learn about the

Japanese-American concentration camps during World War Two, the mistreatment of Indigenous Americans, the Tulsa Massacre, the Chinese Exclusion Act of 1882, Stonewall, etc.

I've been in this fight my entire life because of my skin and now also my sexuality. You have the privilege to ignore that struggle because of yours. I'm glad that you are choosing to be a better person.

Megan said that you were thinking of coming to roller derby on Sunday. If so, then I will see you there.

Regards,
Tasha

She really hoped that Brad wasn't bullshitting her, but she suspected that he was sincere. *He might be an overprivileged douchebag, but he isn't stupid. Some white boys never see life outside of their bubble, some see it and can't handle it, and some see it and it changes them for the better. I think that Brad is part of that third group.*

Work was fascinating. Tasha found herself the center of attention for much of the day. When she wasn't fielding client requests and issues, her co-workers wanted to find out about her girlfriend, how they met, how long they had been dating, etc. She had never shared any of her personal life at work, preferring to let everyone else talk about their own lives instead. When she showed up at the holiday party dressed to the nines and then Megan walked in looking like a goddess (or princess according to Sophia) it had set tongues wagging. It wasn't that Tasha didn't want to talk about her life, she just had never felt like she had anything that she wanted to talk about before.

Weirdly, Kevin seemed to leave her alone all day. It seemed that maybe Megan had really put the fear of goddess in him. Tasha wasn't complaining.

On her commute home, she spent most of the time planning

the next batch of freelance work. She was still focused on that when she opened the door, then the smell hit her. "Please tell me that you're making Indian for dinner again."

"Yes, I am," Megan answered as she dropped the spoon that she was holding and whipped around toward Tasha.

"You're the best—mmpf." Anything else was lost as Megan kissed her thoroughly. "Wow, I missed you, too," she said after they came up for air

"Sorry, I got carried away. I really missed you today. Now, stop distracting me with your—" Megan waved toward her. "—incredible hotness. Oh, and say hi to Sophia. Her schoolwork was all done by the time I got home and I'm very proud of her."

Tasha smiled. "Will do, and thank you." She hung up her coat and took off her boots. "Hey, munchkin, your mom says that you did all of your schoolwork before she got home today. I'm very proud of you!"

"Thank you, Mama Tasha! Mommy really missed you."

"I can tell. I missed you both."

"Me too! I'm glad that Mom is so happy when you're home."

"Aw, you're very sweet, angel. Let me go change and then you can tell me all about your day." Tasha walked into their bedroom, pulling at her clothes.

It's wonderful to come home to family and love. So much better than before.

Tasha opened the bathroom door and an orange blur shot out. "Oh, damn!" She raced back into the living room to find the cats eyeing each other, tails held stiffly in the air. Thankfully, both seemed okay with the other. Nocturne hopped back onto the couch with Sophia while Julius set out to explore. Since all was well in the cat-world, Tasha got changed into something comfortable.

Dinner was excellent and they shared some quiet family time afterwards. Once Sophia was in bed, Megan and Tasha soon followed. Tasha wasn't thrilled about early morning yoga, but it was important to Megan that she try it. Once in the bedroom, Tasha waited to see what Megan's comfort level was compared to last night. After Megan finished brushing her teeth, she walked toward the bed, shedding her shirt on the way.

It seems that she's comfortable with this and I really like that view.

CHAPTER 44
INVISIBLE TOUCH

What was I thinking? Oh yeah, I like early morning yoga.

Megan nudged Tasha, who groaned in complaint. "Come on, my love. You can do this!"

"You say that you love me, yet you make me wake up at this hideous hour."

Tasha might've been complaining, but she was getting up. Megan watched her pick a wedgie as she stumbled toward the bathroom. It was unexpectedly hot. A few minutes later, Megan found herself in the closet with Tasha, who was trying to decide what to wear. She walked up behind Tasha and said, "Sweetheart, do you remember how on Sunday morning you were grabbing my ass without permission?"

"Mmm, yeah, although I seem to recall that you did give me permission later."

"I did. Um, in that spirit, may I grab your ass?"

"Oh, yes. Somehow I'm liking this early morning yoga idea a lot more now. Mmm, I like that. Megan?"

"Yes?"

"If you feel comfortable, then you can put your hands inside my underwear."

"Um. Wow, you have an incredible ass."

Another first, and so good.

"Thank you, but you grabbing it is making it hard to pick what to wear for yoga. Maybe we just do it as we are?"

"That is incredibly tempting, but potentially very awkward if Sophia were to wake up. Wear the red top and those pink pajama shorts. Oh, and Tasha, the next time you grab my ass, you have permission to go under my underwear, too."

Oh, I'm glad that she decided to take me up on that offer right away. Time for an experiment.

Megan turned to face Tasha and kissed her. Megan guided Tasha's hands back to her butt, then reached around to grab Tasha's ass, which she promptly squeezed and fondled while Tasha did the same.

Oh, that is fucking amazing. If she moves her hands a bit forward, then she'll feel just how wet I am. As much as I hate to do this, I need to stop before it gets too far. Brad better sign those damn papers soon.

"Holy shit, you make consent sound so sexy."

"That's because it is, love. And we'll definitely try topless yoga sometime when Sophia isn't around. Now, I picked you something to wear, so you should pick something for me to wear."

Early morning yoga went well. As they lay on their mats after an hour, coming down from their exertions, Tasha said, "Okay, maybe you're right. This felt really good. I think that I'm going to cancel my membership at the yoga studio."

"Good. I was worried that you might fall in love with your yoga instructor."

"Too late, I already have."

"Oh, really? What is that tramp's name?" Megan asked with mock fury.

"Mmm, the tramp's name is Megan," Tasha purred, reaching for her. "That hussy even told me that I could do *this.*" With that, she shoved her hands down the back of Megan's yoga pants. Megan kissed her voraciously and returned the favor.

As enjoyable as this was, they did actually have to work, and Sophia had school. Megan reluctantly broke the kiss and removed her hands from Tasha's butt. "I'm enjoying this way too much. I need to take a shower and then get Sophia going."

"Ugh, why do you have to be so responsible?"

That's a really good question. I want to be irresponsible so badly right now. It's like there is a sauna in my panties. Brad sure as hell never had this effect on me.

"Sorry, it comes with being a mom."

"You are a great mom. So, uh… any chance that I can watch you shower? For science and all."

"Wow, if I had known that early morning yoga made you so horny, I would have suggested it before. Hmm. I guess so, but only for a minute and only for science. You need to get coffee going and feed Nocturne and Julius."

"Just a minute?"

"Don't make me set a timer."

Once they got going, Tuesday flew by. Megan wasn't a huge fan of substitute teaching, but it did give her a chance to learn the city and consider what schools she might want to apply to for a permanent position. That afternoon, she taught Sophia how to make biscuits for a dinner of chicken stew and biscuits. Teaching Sophia how to cook was quickly becoming a favorite activity and she really liked how Tasha was also teaching that to Sophia. Who knows, maybe Sophia would grow up to be a chef.

Megan kissed Tasha within an inch of her life when she got home, then they joined Sophia on the couch so they could all talk about their day while dinner finished cooking. After dinner, Tasha cleaned off the table and did dishes while Megan and Sophia relaxed. Before she was sent to bed, Sophia asked if she could make lasagna for dinner the next day. They both liked this idea, but decided that Megan would supervise, just in case.

Once in bed that evening, Megan asked, "Are you up for early morning yoga tomorrow?"

"Yes. I actually felt really good today."

"I'm so glad. Also, would you like to go out with me on Friday night?"

"Like a date?"

"Yes, I am asking you on a date. I've arranged a sitter for Sophia."

"Our first date! Yes, absolutely yes!"

CHAPTER 45

SINGLE LADIES (PUT A RING ON IT)

The next few days went by quickly for Tasha as she looked forward to her first real date with Megan. Sophia did a really good job with the lasagna, and Megan reported that she only watched while Sophia prepared the whole meal by herself. Megan handled getting the lasagna in and out of the oven for safety reasons, but other than that it was all Sophia. They both knew that lasagna looks like it is harder to make than it is, but they were very proud of her for trying it and doing well. She even made garlic bread and a simple salad for their meal.

Work was relatively smooth that week as well. Kevin eventually got over his fear of Megan, but Tasha was more than capable of handling whatever bullshit projects he gave her. Her co-workers seemed more open and engaging with her now that she opened up to them. She still didn't love the job, but that was more about the corporate BS than the actual work—she felt much more engaged when she was at home doing freelance work. Lauren's contacts were paying off, and now those contacts were referring people to her as well.

The best parts of her week, though, were those involving Megan and Sophia. Her daily walks to school with Sophia and their chats about her day had become an important ritual in her own life. As for Megan, she felt like they were both getting more comfortable with just being together.

Friday morning, Tasha wore an ankle-length skirt and a festive yet classy sweater, as well as a long coat, because Megan had told her that they would be going out for dinner right after work. Megan scored tickets to a play from another teacher whose plans had changed and couldn't go.

Tasha got to the brewpub first, but she didn't have to wait long. Her girlfriend arrived moments later, dressed in a classy but not overly elegant outfit for their date. They kissed and sat down at their table and chatted about their day as they perused the menu. It was a comfort food night with Tasha choosing a hearty stew and Megan going with the mac and cheese. Each paired their entree with one of the suggested beers. Once they ordered and their beers arrived, they sat back and relaxed a bit.

Megan restarted the conversation. "Next week is going to be interesting, and probably pretty weird."

"Right… Next week was supposed to be a holiday week, right?"

"Yeah. A lot of teachers will be out because they already had plans. Other school staff as well. I have no idea how this will all work."

"Does the school district even know?"

"Not a clue as far as I can tell. Because I'm a sub, I'm getting time and a half all of next week, but regular teachers don't."

"That's messed up! How did that happen?"

"The district insisted on that when the strike was ending."

"That seems stupid and unfair and a good way to piss people off."

"Yep, all three. I mean, at this point, most people have reached the acceptance stage, and I'm not complaining about the extra money, but wow… it's definitely messed up."

"Are you still going to see about going permanent in PPS?"

"Yeah, it makes the most sense. I'm looking at the current openings, and I figure that there could be some more openings in the new year. I'm back at McDaniel High School all of next week. I really liked the vibe there, so I'm happy about that."

"That's good. Any other schools that you like?"

"Almost all of them so far. Irvington was really nice. I liked Richmond, but that's the Japanese language magnet and I don't speak Japanese, so probably not. I dunno, I'm keeping an open mind."

"That's good. Tell me if there's anything I can do to support you."

"You mean besides being the best girlfriend that a woman could ask for? Hey, speaking of support, is there anything that I can do to support you?"

Wow, she really is amazing.

"What do you mean?"

"Well, you've been doing a lot of freelance work in the evenings, plus your regular job. Then I've got you doing early morning yoga now…"

"Not gonna lie, the extra work is… It's good and I really enjoy it, but every time I finish a project, that person seems to find me two or three new clients. So far, I haven't had to say no, and it's a good problem to have, but…" Tasha shrugged to accentuate the potential dilemma.

"You're good at what you do, and that's awesome, but you might be reaching your limit."

"Yeah. Exactly."

"Have you thought about quitting your job and going freelance full-time?"

"Pretty much every day. I need health insurance, though. Which sucks. I guess I could take a look at what's out there again and see if I can afford it plus rent and all."

"Hmmm, there might be another option." Megan's face brightened as she was talking, and Tasha leaned forward in anticipation.

"What's that?"

"Substitutes get health insurance and while I wasn't a sub last school year, I was a full-time teacher and worked the required number of hours, in another district, of course. Anyway, I'm finally getting insurance and I should be able to get you on mine as a domestic partner. Let me check."

They both whipped out their phones and started searching. Megan was slightly faster to find the answer. "Well, we meet all of the requirements except one."

Tasha caught up. "You're still married."

"Yeah. I wonder if the fact that I've filed divorce papers will get around that."

"It wouldn't hurt to ask. We may also see Brad at roller derby on Sunday."

"True... I don't want to get into a big fight in front of a crowd. And he may not show up."

"I think he'll show up. He emailed me a few days ago about some books that I told him to read. He said that he was planning to come because of Sophia."

"Wait... you and Brad have been emailing?" Megan's tone sounded more concerned than surprised.

"Sorry, I should have mentioned it before. I told him to read a couple of books to help him pull his head out of his ass. That was part of my conditions for not giving him the bad envelope. Anyway, he read the books and we emailed back and forth a bit. I decided that he could keep the good envelope."

"That's... good, I guess."

"It is. He's still an asshole, but I think he might be having a bit of personal growth."

"Huh."

"You aren't having second thoughts, are you?" Tasha experienced a sudden flash of anxiety.

"Oh, about Brad? Hell, no! No, he and I are done, outside of the fact that he's Sophia's father. I've found the love of my life with someone else, and even if Brad does change, he can't change that."

'Love of her life.' I like the sound of that.

"Really? He sounds like a lucky guy." Tasha grinned.

Megan grinned right back. "This might surprise you, but I think that she's a lucky girl. Not nearly as lucky as me, though."

"Tell me more. Is she hot?"

"Super hot. Smart, too. And she's good with Sophia."

"Wow, she sounds almost as amazing as you."

"She is… I, um…"

Come on, Megan. The suspense is killing me. We were playful and now she's serious.

"What?"

"I want to spend the rest of my life with her."

"Wow, she is a lucky girl."

"…and, um. There's something that I haven't told her, though. Something that I just realized myself."

Tasha suddenly felt very alert. "What's that?"

"I think… um, I think that I want to marry her."

"Holy shit! Megan, are you sure?"

Megan blushed and said, "Yes. Not immediately. I think that I need a couple of months after my divorce, but yes, I want to marry you, Tasha."

Tasha practically leapt over the table to shower Megan with kisses. Their waitress arrived with their food right about then. "Wow, I can come back if you need a minute."

Tasha quickly composed herself and said, "No, that's okay. Sorry about that. My girlfriend just told me that she wants to marry me."

"Congratulations! I'm guessing that was a yes, then."

"Uh, yeah. Definitely yes."

"That's awesome! Watch out for the mac and cheese, the bowl is hot. You two enjoy your dinner now!" With that, the waitress gave them a wink and was off.

Getting married was never a priority for me and now it's suddenly all I want. Same with raising a child.

They dug into their meals, each contemplating recent events.

Tasha broke the silence first. "Since you said it, I feel that I need to say it as well, even though we both know it. I want to marry you, Megan. Does this mean that we're engaged now?"

"I'm not sure. I think so. I honestly wasn't expecting this, but then we were talking about being domestic partners, and I realized that wasn't enough for me. If I'm going to be with you, then I'm going to be all in. That's what you deserve."

Tasha smiled. "That's what we both deserve. I do recall something about rings, though."

"Yes, I did promise to put a ring on your finger."

"Mmm, no diamonds, though. I want a ruby, set in silver. And you need a ring, too."

"Oh, I like the silver idea. An emerald, set in silver for me."

"That's perfect. Would you like to pick them out together?"

"I would love to pick out rings together. What do you think of matching settings?"

Tasha briefly considered that before saying, "I think that would be adorable."

"There is just one problem, though. I'm still married right now."

"Well, if Brad won't sign the divorce papers, then I have two good reasons to rip his arms off and beat him to death with them."

"What's the other—oh!" Megan's face turned scarlet.

"I mean… only when you are ready and feel comfortable. I will wait for you for as long as it takes, because you are worth it."

"Um… maybe we could each rip off one of Brad's arms and beat him to death with them."

"Oh, Goddess. You are so hot when you talk like that."

Megan laughed. The waitress cycled back, asking how their meals were and if they needed more to drink. Once they were done, she cleared the table. The waitress came back with a brownie sundae complete with two lit candles. "Congratulations again on your engagement. If you have any allergies, then I can get something else."

"This is perfect, and very thoughtful. Thank you so much!"

"You're very welcome! Enjoy, you two!"

"We're going to need to put in some extra yoga time tomorrow for this."

"Worth it. So worth it."

CHAPTER 46
C'MON LET'S GO

Megan groaned at the alarm, but her groan lacked energy. She wasn't used to having an early alarm on Saturday. *Wait for it.* Tasha pounced on her, sending poor Julius scrambling off in a huff toward Sophia's room.

"Megan," Tasha purred. "Are you ready for yoga?"

"You know, I recall that you once accused me of being a monster, and now it seems that I've created a monster instead."

Tasha nibbled gently on her ear. "I'll let you pick out what I should wear…" They had been playing that game every morning and it was very fun.

"Mmm, but I like your current outfit."

"I know, and I like your current outfit, but I should remind you that you're the one with the 'No Topless Yoga' rule."

"Ugh, why do I do this to myself?"

"Um, why do you do this to us is the better question?" Tasha was moving down from her earlobe to her neck.

Goddess, that feels amazing.

Megan was struggling to form coherent thoughts or words. This problem didn't get any easier when she felt Tasha's tongue tracing her jawline before moving up her chin to her mouth. Megan surrendered to the kisses.

Eventually, she reluctantly pushed Tasha away. "You were the one who insisted on early morning yoga on a Saturday."

Tasha pouted at her.

"Maybe we could lock the door and do yoga in here. I think there's enough space."

Tasha practically bounced with glee. "Let me check!" Tasha raced for the closet to grab the mats. "They fit, mostly. We can't be side-by-side, but that could have benefits…"

"Lock the door then, and I guess we'll be doing topless yoga." Megan watched Tasha do a happy dance.

I never really thought about getting a tattoo, but those really are amazing works of art. I'll have to check with Sophia first, though.

Tasha's happy dance wound down, and Megan watched as Tasha hooked her thumbs into the waistband of her panties.

"You know, Megan, since we're already ninety percent of the way there…" Megan groaned as she watched Tasha's arms inch tantalizingly downward. "Oh, Goddess."

I'm not sure which is sexier, watching Tasha jump up and down while topless, or watching her slowly tease her panties down. We saw each other naked in college, but this is so much better. And now she is turning around for me. She has to know what this is doing to me.

I'm going to murder Brad if he doesn't sign those papers. Focus, Megan. It's time to tease Tasha a bit.

"You mean like this?" With that, Megan hooked her thumbs into her own waistband and started a slow, sensual shimmy as she lowered her panties. On instinct, she turned and looked over her shoulder as she bent to drag them down to her feet. Megan could see that Tasha was transfixed.

Mmmm, that's the reaction that I wanted.

The first few minutes of their nude yoga session was a mixture of self-confident poses, leering, and awkward stretching. After a few minutes, the routine kicked in and their state of undress became mostly background noise. Mostly.

Feeling invigorated and sweaty, they finished their yoga session and were staring openly at each other in lotus poses.

Megan felt extraordinarily confident, even as she was completely exposed.

"Tasha, I need to tell you something."

It looked like Tasha was trying to focus on her eyes but struggling to maintain contact. "What's that?"

"I am soaking wet right now, and I'm not talking about yoga sweat."

"Megan, that makes two of us."

Megan watched Tasha's hand move down to touch herself and then come back up with visual evidence of just how turned on Tasha was.

"As much as I really want to take care of that for you, I still can't, you know, because of the marriage thing. I do have an idea though."

Tasha was panting, and Megan could only assume that it wasn't from their recent exertions. Megan continued, "I think that now would be an excellent time to see how big that shower is."

"Hell, yes." Tasha jumped to her feet, grabbed Megan's hand, and Megan felt herself being dragged toward the shower.

As much as the two of them enjoyed their shower, they had to eventually bring it to a close. It was time to get ready as they had a big surprise for Sophia today. Megan checked on her daughter and found her sleeping soundly, sandwiched between two cats. While Tasha showered, she put out food and fresh water for Nocturne and Julius. Tasha fixed human breakfast while Megan showered and the cats ate. Megan got Sophia up and moving while Tasha made a run for three hot chocolates as neither of them felt like they needed coffee after their morning.

Sophia's mood brightened up with the hot chocolate. "Hey, sweetheart. Tasha and I have a surprise for you."

"What is it?"

"If we tell you, it won't be a surprise, will it? Once you finish your breakfast, we'll get our coats on and go for a drive."

It was a short drive to a scouting fundraiser tree lot. As she parked, Megan said to Sophia, "Sweetheart, would you like to help us pick out a Christmas tree?"

"Yes, Mommy!" It took extra effort to get Sophia unhooked as she was very excited.

Megan and Tasha strolled hand-in-hand through the tree lot, watching Sophia bounce excitedly from tree to tree. Megan leaned in and asked, "Are you sure that you're okay with this?"

"Me? I'm fine. I hope that the cats don't go crazy. You've seen those videos, right?"

Megan laughed. "Oh, yeah! I'm hoping that as well. You're an atheist and I don't want to…"

"Baby, it's okay. Like I said, I may not believe, but *this*," Tasha gestured to themselves and Sophia, "this is what I care about. Look at that girl. She is over the moon about this. Spending time with you and her, with friends, that's what is important to me. The 25th of December was just a random day picked to compete with an ancient pagan holiday. This tree that we're picking out is a recycled Germanic pagan tradition. I don't care about none of that. I care about that big ol' smile on our little girl's face."

"Sorry, I just wanted to be sure. And I liked that you said 'our little girl.'"

"I appreciate that. I do. And you know… ever since I saw you walk into that holiday party in that green and silver dress, like Brigid herself, I've started to think that the problem is that men screwed up religion, as usual, and that goddesses are real and where it's at."

"Who is Brigid?"

"Are you sure that you're Irish? She's the ancient Irish goddess of poetry, healing, wisdom, and the forge. Absolute badass who of course got christianized into a sappy saint."

"I don't have your classical background, but you've definitely got some goddess in you."

And I'd like to put some goddess in you, too. Okay, down girl.

"Don't you forget it! Hey, munchkin! Did you find a tree that you like?"

"Yes, Mama Tasha! I think that this is our tree!"

The tree seemed fresh enough to last a few weeks. There was a bit of a bare patch, but placing it in a corner would fix that problem. They talked to the nice Scout mom in charge and got the tree loaded on top of the car. They also purchased a stand and some light strings.

Once home, Megan and Tasha maneuvered the tree into place, much to the interest and amusement of Nocturne and Julius. Within minutes, the lower branches of the tree were decorated with the four golden orbs of the two cats. "I hope that doesn't become a problem," Megan said to Tasha.

"You and me both! I'm hoping that they get bored of it soon."

As a family, they strung up lights and hung some wooden ornaments. The tree looked good, but a bit barren. Sophia suggested that they cut out paper snowflakes and hang those. Megan and Sophia worked on that while Tasha did some freelance work close by. By the time that they were done, the cats had settled in on the couch with Tasha, so Megan and Sophia hung up the snowflakes while Tasha supervised from afar.

They spent much of the rest of the day on the couch, Tasha working, Megan and Sophia reading, Nocturne and Julius snuggling the humans.

CHAPTER 47
BABA O'RILEY

Later that night, once Sophia was in bed, Tasha noticed a marked deterioration in Megan's mood. She seemed withdrawn, and their usual playful banter and looks as they prepared themselves for bed was missing. Megan even kept her shirt on as she climbed into bed. Instead of getting in bed herself, Tasha sat down on the edge of the bed near Megan and said, "Is it something that you feel comfortable talking about?"

"What?"

"Whatever is bothering you."

"There's noth—it's Brad. I haven't seen him in what… three weeks? I'm really anxious about seeing him again tomorrow."

"What about that is making you anxious?

"I don't really know. Maybe because he was such an asshole the last time I saw him. Maybe I'm just worried that Sophia will see him and decide that she'd rather be with him."

"She did choose you…"

And me.

"I know, it's irrational and stupid."

"It's not. It's human nature. Hey, I just want you to know that I'm here for you."

"Thank you, Tasha. Can you hold me?"

"Of course, my love." Tasha lay down and Megan cuddled in. They stayed like that for a long time, until they fell asleep.

Tasha woke up around midnight with a crick in her neck and a wet spot on her shirt. She tried to extricate herself from Megan's grasp without waking her girlfriend but failed. "Sweetheart, I'm sorry. My neck hurts and I have to pee."

"I'm sorry, too. Was I snoring?"

"Yes, like a small bear."

Megan wiped at her mouth. "Oh no, was I drooling?"

"Um, yeah." Tasha giggled, "I like it better when you drool over me and not on me."

"You know, if your shirt is wet, you should probably take it off." Megan waggled her eyebrows.

"You're incorrigible," Tasha said as she stripped off the damp garment. "Okay, I really gotta pee!"

Tasha noted that Megan's shirt was on the floor when she exited the bathroom, but all that she could see was the purplish-red mop of Megan's hair poking out from under the sheets. Tasha slid into bed and reached for her light.

"Ta-sha… If I told you that you have nice boobs, would you hold them against me?"

If I start that, then I know exactly how I'll finish it, so I better not, at least tonight. Brad better have those papers signed, or I'm going to beat him.

"Goodnight, Megan."

Megan's anxiety seemed to have ebbed by the time they woke up. Early morning yoga and a good breakfast helped. Tasha got Sophia up a bit earlier than usual. "Sophia, today I'm going to teach you how I make chili. Do you know what makes chili so special?"

"No, Mama Tasha."

"Because every chili is different. It's one of the most personal dishes that someone can make."

"Why is that?"

"Because every person is different. I like mine spicy with about an even mix of meat and beans. Some people make sweet chili. Some people make all-meat chili. Some people make vegan chili. As you grow up, you'll try different chilis and find out what you like. Then you'll start making your own. You will tinker and adjust until your chili suits you. As you grow older and change, your chili will change, too."

"That's awesome, Mama Tasha! Are all foods like that?"

"Many are, but some lend themselves to individual creativity better than others. Some foods should only be done a certain way."

Megan had clearly been eavesdropping, because her voice floated in, saying, "Like vinegar-based barbeque sauce!"

"Girl! You know that is heresy! Mustard-based is the only proper form of barbeque sauce." Tasha's native South Carolina accent appeared in full force. She could hear Megan's crystal clear laughter. Megan had known her for over fourteen years and knew just what pushing that particular button would do. Sophia looked confused.

"Munchkin, your mommy likes to tease your Mama Tasha by saying horrible, nasty things. But Mama Tasha is gonna get her back by teaching you the true form of barbeque. Once you've tasted a true South Carolina mustard-based barbeque sauce, you'll know that anything else is just a cheap imitation of the real thing."

"Okay, I trust you, Mama Tasha."

"Good girl!"

"How come you don't measure?"

"That's a good question, munchkin. When you are first learning to make something, a recipe can be very helpful. But when you know something deep in your bones, like I know my chili, you can just feel it."

"Wow… Can I cook like that?"

"One day, angel, you will. You did so good with that lasagna! Practice some more and get comfortable in the kitchen. You'll get there. Cooking is a good skill to have. I've had to feed myself for years and being able to cook has made that much better."

I'm going to teach you everything, little angel, because you are family now.

Tasha smiled at Sophia and she returned it with an impish grin.

Lunch was chili over rice, with cheese and sour cream. It was delicious, and Megan promised to show Sophia how she made chili, because she liked to add cinnamon and cocoa to hers.

After lunch, it was off to roller derby. Tasha held Megan's hand tightly as they entered, reassuring her with that solid grip. Brad was already there and waved.

"Daddy!" And with that, Sophia was off like a shot.

Megan and Tasha followed at a more leisurely pace. Tasha could feel Megan's tension beside her. Brad looked at them and said, "Hello."

"Hello," they said back, each with a cold edge on her voice.

"I'm guessing that this is official now," Brad said, glancing at their hands. Tasha could feel Megan's spine stiffen and heard the steel in her voice. "It is."

Brad smiled, although Tasha could see a hint of sadness there. "I'm very happy for you both. You were always perfect for each other. I'm just sorry that… Well, I'm sorry for a lot of things."

"And you should be."

"Megan, I have a lot to apologize for, but maybe we can just focus on Sophia for right now. I want to know all about this sport that she is so interested in."

Megan and Tasha sat behind Brad and Sophia as she tried to explain what they were about to see. Once it started, she was locked in and so was Brad. Megan and Tasha half watched the game, half watched the two in front of them. At halftime, all the kids in the audience were invited onto the track to play with hula hoops and tricycles and to just run around and burn off energy.

Brad turned around and said, "I'm sorry if I made you feel uncomfortable. I truly am happy for you. Both of you."

Megan was keeping quiet, so Tasha said, "Thanks, Brad."

"I, um… I signed the papers, Megan. There's one change, and I think that you'll be okay with it."

Megan responded, "What's that?"

"I'm selling the house, and I want you to have half."

"Why?"

"Before I answer, who the hell is your lawyer? Because my guy shit his pants when he saw her name on the documents."

I bet he did. Maria is pure badass.

Tasha fielded this, saying, "She's a good friend of mine, and now a friend of Megan and Sophia's, too."

"She must be one heckuva divorce lawyer. My guy told me that I was screwed. Then he read it and said that I was lucky to have my balls still attached."

"Yeah, that was the bad envelope…"

"Thank you for not giving me that."

Megan jumped in, "And say thank you to me, too. Maria only wanted one document, but I insisted on two."

"Yes, thank you, Megan. I didn't deserve it." Tasha nodded vigorously in agreement.

"You deserve much better than me, and I'm glad that you found her," Brad said. "Sophia deserves better, too. More than anything, I want to be the person that she thinks that I am."

"That would be an improvement for sure," Tasha commented.

"So, about the house. I got a job with a credit union, up near Seattle. Tasha, you were right about me. I've always had my father telling me what to do, where to go, what job to have. I'm good at what I do, or at least I think I am. Now I get to find out for sure. Maybe I'll take cooking classes or learn how to make kombucha. Figure out who I am."

Imagine that. Good for you Brad. Not that I'm about to say that.

Megan said, "That's good, Brad. I'm happy for you and I wish you the best."

"Thanks, Megan. I… thank you."

They sat there in an awkward silence before Brad asked, "I

thought there would be more… contact, I guess. Am I missing something?"

Tasha answered, "It's the age group. The Rose Petals are the youngest skaters and they have rules that strictly limit contact. Around 12, they move up to the Rose Buds, and there's more contact there."

"That's the next one, right?"

"Yes."

"Cool! Um, Megan. I want to thank you for this, too. You could have enrolled Sophia in this without me, and I really appreciate that you included me in this... That you included me in something that has captured Sophia's interest. I am really excited to see her skate. I mean, if you are, of course."

"I'm excited to see her skate, too. Maybe we can both tell her together that she can try out."

"I'd really like that, thank you. Oh, one last thing. With me selling the house and all, I packed up your clothes and stuff, and Sophia's. It's all in the back of my truck. I figured that you wouldn't want to drive all that way and I was coming here anyway…"

"Thank you, Brad."

The rest of the afternoon actually went really well. Megan and Tasha moved down during intermission so that Sophia was between her two parents. In the Buds game, the crowd went nuts when the jammer with the derby name, Harley Quinn, jumped over the apex of the track.

Tasha smiled as she watched Sophia's glee and how that excitement spread to both Brad and Megan as they imagined their little girl doing the same thing one day.

After they unloaded Brad's truck, Tasha surprised herself by suggesting that they all go out for dinner. It was much more pleasant than she would have thought possible at the start of the day. Sophia went to bed early, as she was exhausted by the day's excitement.

Tasha slipped into bed and prepared to turn off the light once

Megan joined her.

Where did she go anyway?

Then the closet door opened and Megan emerged wearing something lacy and gauzy and delectably sinful.

"Tasha..." Megan purred seductively. "Brad signed the papers..."

AFTERWORD
ANGEL

The next day, Tasha put in her two weeks notice. Lauren was thrilled to send her a bunch of potential new clients. When she heard about their relationship, Lauren sent another gift basket. Megan found a permanent position for the next school year at one of her favorite schools.

Megan and Tasha planned to have a quiet wedding on Memorial Day weekend. It was a small, intimate ceremony with a few friends and family. They even invited Brad as a courtesy.

He was coming with his girlfriend, Devika. They met at a yoga class and had been dating for a few months. With Megan's permission, he wanted to introduce Sophia to Devika.

Nocturne and Julius enjoyed napping on or near their humans and occasionally chasing each other wildly around the apartment. Sophia was making friends and enjoying her school.

Tasha joined the PTA. Sophia went to a junior roller derby boot camp and started skating. She would be on one of the home teams in the fall. Sophia was over the moon when Megan announced that she was planning to join the Rose City Rollers recreational team. Sophia was already dreaming that maybe one day she could play with her mom.

TASHA AND MEGAN'S PLAYLIST

Road To Nowhere - Ozzy Ozbourne
You've Got a Friend in Me - Randy Newman
Crying in the Rain - Whitesnake
The Best - Tina Turner
Gimme Shelter - Rolling Stones
Cinnamon Girl - Neil Young
Wild Wild Life - Talking Heads
Push It - Salt-N-Pepa
Manic Monday - The Bangles
9 to 5 - Dolly Parton
Telephone - Lady Gaga, Beyoncé
Girls Just Wanna Have Fun - Cyndi Lauper
Joyride - Roxette
Can't Take My Eyes Off Of You - Dirty Looks
What Is Love - Haddaway
Saturday Night's Alright (For Fighting) - Elton John
Sympathy For the Devil - Rolling Stones
Fortress Around Your Heart - Sting
Cold as Ice - Foreigner
You Belong With Me - Taylor Swift
Venus - Bananarama
We Found Love - Rihanna, Calvin Harris
I Want To Know What Love Is - Foreigner
That's What Friends Are For - Dionne Warwick with Elton John, Gladys
Knight, & Stevie Wonder
All I Want For Christmas is You - Mariah Carey
Cold Shower - Kix
Switch 625 - Def Leppard
Every Rose Has Its Thorn - Poison
Listen To Your Heart - Roxette
Heaven and Hell - Black Sabbath
New Attitude - Patti LaBelle
Under Pressure - Queen with David Bowie
It's All Coming Back To Me Now - Celine Dion
One Night in Bangkok - Murray Head
In Your Eyes - Peter Gabriel
This Kiss - Faith Hill

Take Me Home Tonight / Be My Baby - Eddie Money with Ronnie Spector
I Kissed A Girl - Jill Sobule
Confident - Demi Lovato
I'd Do Anything For Love (But I Won't Do That) - Meatloaf
You're the First, the Last, My Everything - Barry White
Dream On - Aerosmith
Invisible Touch - Genesis
Single Ladies (Put A Ring On It) - Beyoncé
C'Mon Let's Go - Girlschool
Baba O'Riley - The Who
Angel - Aerosmith
No One Like You - Scorpions

https://open.spotify.com/playlist/3RkDMNFgE6N4zI5rpWyXNd?si=
e5c06e3878c64749

ACKNOWLEDGMENTS

I would like to first thank my good friend, Steve Davala. He was the one who challenged me to try to write a book. We agreed to hold each other accountable for pushing ourselves to write. To both of our surprises, this book came out of my head in less than three weeks. The rest of the process took much longer.

I would also like to thank my wife, Cecily. Not only has she been supportive throughout this entire process, she is also an excellent editor. Speaking of editing, I also want to thank Francesca Varela for her help with editing, and helping me be a better writer.

I should also thank our cats, Merlin, Lady Starlight, and of course, the dearly departed Francesca. All three of them helped shape Nocturne and Julius.

Thank you to my brave alpha readers, who knew that I was a first-time author and agreed to read this anyway.

And also thank you to all of the independent authors out there. I've received a lot of support and advice from this community as I work toward getting a book from an unrealized dream to a physical thing of ink and paper.

ABOUT THE AUTHOR

Chris Walters lives in Portland, Oregon with his wife and two cats. When not reading, writing, or working, he is a roller derby announcer for the Rose City Rollers.

Follow him on Instagram at @cwaltersauthor or visit his website at www.chriswaltersauthor.com

www.ingramcontent.com/pod-product-compliance
Lightning Source LLC
Chambersburg PA
CBHW060444310726

48977CB00001B/311